## "What have you told him about me?"

She sucked in her breath. "Very little."

"Even so, could you spell it out for me?"

Suddenly she jerked her head in his direction. Those gorgeous brown eyes pierced his with laserlike intensity. "You mean the way you spelled it out for me?" she cried. Her hands had gripped the steering wheel with enough force he imagined she could bend it. "I told him the truth—that you didn't love me after all. That was all I knew to tell him. It's all he knows."

Theo studied her features. "Yet you left out half the story. It's time he heard that *you* stopped loving me. I'm sure he has no idea that you never intended to come to the church and go away with me, so we could be married and have our baby in peace."

The blood seemed to drain out of her face. "I was there. I waited for hours." Her voice throbbed.

Theo was incredulous. "That's an interesting fairy tale. Take a look." He handed the returned letter he'd sent to her. "If you're ever curious enough to read what's on the inside of the envelope, then you'll know my state of mind at the time. In the meantime, I'm here to claim what's mine—Ari."

Dear Reader,

Jilted at the altar!

An old phrase that still puts a dagger into our hearts—because we know that when it happens *someone* is suffering the most agonizing pain.

In *The Greek's Long-Lost Son,* Stella Athas undergoes this life-changing experience. Then, just as she gets her life together and things are going well, the man who shattered her heart and her dreams makes a sudden dramatic appearance, informing her he's never going away again.

Her first instinct is to run from him—but where? It isn't that easy when neither of them wants to hurt the adorable six-year-old son they made together. How would *you,* the reader, have handled this situation? Find out what Stella did.

Enjoy!

*Rebecca Winters*

ww.cleanromances.com

# REBECCA WINTERS

## The Greek's
## Long-Lost Son

ESCAPE
AROUND
the
WORLD

# HARLEQUIN®

TORONTO • NEW YORK • LONDON
AMSTERDAM • PARIS • SYDNEY • HAMBURG
STOCKHOLM • ATHENS • TOKYO • MILAN • MADRID
PRAGUE • WARSAW • BUDAPEST • AUCKLAND

Recycling programs
for this product may
not exist in your area.

ISBN-13: 978-0-373-17615-1

THE GREEK'S LONG-LOST SON

First North American Publication 2009.

Copyright © 2009 by Rebecca Winters.

This edition published by arrangement with Harlequin Books S.A.

® and TM are trademarks of the publisher. Trademarks indicated with
® are registered in the United States Patent and Trademark Office, the
Canadian Trade Marks Office and in other countries.

www.eHarlequin.com

**Printed in U.S.A.**

A very loyal fan who read one of my
Greek romances, *If He Could See Me Now,* urged
me to write Stella's story. Stella was a member
of the powerful Athas Greek shipping family and a
secondary character in the book. How lucky am I
to have readers who get hooked on a novel
and want to know more?


Stella's story,
*The Greek's Long-Lost Son,*
is for you, BUFFER, with my gratitude!

# CHAPTER ONE

AFTER a hard day's work negotiating prices with their overseas clients, Stella Athas left her office at the Athens headquarters a little after three o'clock in her new white Jaguar XK convertible, the first car she'd ever owned. Until she'd bought it with her own money two months ago, she'd used the old clunker estate car to get around.

Along with her new purchase, it seemed a different hairdo was necessary too. She'd always worn her dark hair long and straight, but all that had changed with the convertible, because the whole point of having the top down was to feel the sun and the breeze. It had only taken one day of whizzing around in it looking like the head of a mop for Stella to go to a beauty salon and get her hair cut in a trendy jaw-length style.

Everyone seemed to approve of her new look. Her colleagues said it emphasized the high cheekbones of her oval face. Her friends insisted it brought out the velvety texture of her midnight-brown eyes.

Her oldest brother, Stasio, teased her that she'd better watch out; she was a great beauty like their deceased mother. All the men, eligible or otherwise, had their eye on her now that she'd been seen around Athens in her flashy new sports car. When was she going to get serious over Keiko and take him for a ride in it? Didn't she know she was breaking his heart?

Stella knew that her brother was hoping she and Keiko Pappas would get together, but she'd been too burned by an experience in her past to get into an intimate relationship with another man. She preferred to remain friends with Keiko or any other guy hoping to get close to her for that matter.

As for today, she didn't want to think about anything but having fun because this marked the beginning of her three-week vacation from work. It was also the end of the school year for her six-year-old son, Ari.

Although she liked the family's town villa in Athens well enough—after all, it had been home to the Athas clan for three generations—she was a beach girl at heart and always looked forward to their holidays on Andros with Stasio and his wife, Rachel.

When Stella had attended college in New York, she'd met an American girl named Rachel Maynard. They had become best friends at a time when Stella had been recovering from what she could only look back on now as a nervous breakdown. When Theo Pantheras had deserted her and their unborn child, she'd allowed it to almost destroy her. Of course, that had been six years ago. She'd long since recovered, but the experience had caused her to lose her faith in men.

Still, with a vacation looming, none of that mattered now. She was eager to join Rachel, who'd married Stasio and who now had two little daughters, Cassie and Zoe, who adored Ari and he them. Everyone was looking forward to being together at the family villa on Andros and at some point her brother Nikos would be arriving from Switzerland with his wife Renate to vacation with them, too.

Nikos's arrival was always a worry for Stella, because he had a nasty temper and could make life difficult when he wanted to. Hopefully, this time he'd be on his best behavior, but she didn't know if it was possible.

Rather than be flown in Stasio's helicopter, Stella planned to drive her and Ari this visit. She wanted the new car at her disposal as she sped around the island and enjoyed the glorious summer. Tomorrow morning they'd leave early and take the ferry from Rafina. Ari loved ships of all kinds and adored being on the water. So did she and couldn't wait to get away from the city. It was starting to get overcrowded with tourists.

Once she'd pulled around the back of the house, she parked away from the trees and birds and hurried through the screened-in back porch where deliveries were left. When she entered the big kitchen, she saw the elderly housekeeper watering a plant at the sink.

"*Yiasas,* Iola. How was your day?"

She turned her gray head to look at Stella. "Busy."

"Cheer up. Ari and I will be leaving in the morning. With Stasio's family out of here, too, you'll have three weeks to take it easy and enjoy yourself." Stella gave her a kiss on the cheek. "I'm going upstairs to get packed."

"Everything has been washed and dried. You want me to bring up the luggage?"

"Thank you, but my suitcase is already in my closet. We don't need to take that much to the beach. Mine will hold both our things."

Grabbing an apple from the basket, she took a big bite and headed for the staircase at the front of the house. When they weren't on Andros, Stasio and Rachel lived at the villa on the third floor with the girls, she and Ari on the second. Nikos's suite was on the first floor next to the pool, but he was rarely here.

Once she entered her suite adjoining Ari's, she got to work. Ari had gone to spend the day with his school friend Dax, and Stella planned to pick him up at his friend's house around four-thirty. That gave her an hour.

While she started gathering tops, shorts and swimsuits for both of them, the house phone rang once. She picked up the receiver at her bedside table. "What is it, Iola?"

"You need to come downstairs. The postman has a registered letter for you that only you can sign."

Stella frowned. "Anything legal goes to Stasio's office, but you already know that."

"I told him, but he said this one is for you. He insists he has to deliver it into your hands, no one else's."

The postman could have done that while Stella had still been at the office. "I'll be right down."

What on earth was going on? Stella hung up the phone, eager to straighten out what was obviously a mistake so she could finish her packing. She hurried downstairs to the foyer and entered the front room.

*"Yiasou."*

The postman nodded. "You are Despinis Estrella Athas?"

"Yes." But no one ever addressed her by her birth name.

He thrust a clipboard at her. "Please sign the card on the bottom line to prove this was delivered to you personally."

"May I ask who sent it?"

"I have no idea."

Despite her irritation, Stella smiled while she wrote down her signature. "Don't shoot the messenger, right?"

But her comment was wasted on the postman, who remained stoic.

He took the clipboard and handed her the letter. "I'll see myself out."

Iola followed him to the front door and shut it behind him. Stella wandered into the foyer, more bemused than anything else by the interruption. "Perhaps I got caught speeding in my new car by one of those traffic cameras. You think?" Stella quipped.

"Aren't you going to open it and find out?"

Stella had waited too long for her vacation to be bothered by anything now. "Maybe after I get back from our trip. After all, if this had been brought to the door tomorrow, I wouldn't have been here."

"But you signed for it today!"

"True. Why don't you open it and tell me what it says while I finish packing." She handed it to Iola before starting up the stairs to make inroads on her packing.

Stella fully expected the housekeeper to come rushing after her with the news, yet no such thing happened. In fact it was eerily quiet. After a few minutes Stella stepped out in the hall and walked to the head of the stairs.

"Iola?"

Total silence.

"Iola?" Stella called in a louder voice.

When nothing was forthcoming she raced down the stairs. No sign of her in the salon. "Iola?" She ran through the house to the kitchen, where she found her sitting on one of the kitchen chairs, her head in her hands. The letter lay open on the table.

As she started to reach for it, Iola grabbed it from her and pressed it to her ample bosom. "No! This is not for your eyes."

The loyal housekeeper had been with their family since Stella had been in elementary school. She knew everything that went on under their roof. Stella had no doubt Iola would defend her to the death if the situation warranted it.

"What's so terrible you don't want me to see it?" Her question was met with quiet sobs. Stella sat down on the chair next to her and put a loving arm around her heaving shoulders. "Iola? Please. Let me see it."

A minute passed before she handed Stella the one-page letter. Her eyes fell on the missive. It was hand-written in bold, decisive strokes that looked faintly familiar. Stella's heart skipped a beat.

Dear Stella:
It's been a long time since the last time we were together. After the letters I sent you came back unopened and I'd exhausted every possibility of finding you, I left for New York to work, but now I'm back in Athens for good.

I saw you walking near your villa with a boy who has Pantheras written all over him. He's my flesh and blood, too.

You and I need to meet.

I can be reached at the phone number on my office letterhead. I've also written my cell phone number here. I'll expect your call tomorrow before the day is out. Don't make me petition the court to secure my right to be with my son. That's the last thing I would want to do to either of you.

Theo.

Stella's cry reverberated against the walls of the kitchen.

As she read the letter again, Theo's name swam

before her eyes. She started to get up from the chair, but her body began to feel icy. Nausea rendered her too weak to stand. There was a ringing in her ears. In the distance she heard Iola cry before she felt herself slump against the housekeeper.

When next she had any cognizance of her surroundings, she discovered she was lying on the kitchen floor. Iola was leaning over her whispering prayers while she patted Stella's cheeks with a cold, wet cloth. As the housekeeper fussed over her, a memory of the letter filled her mind.

After six years Theo Pantheras had reappeared in her life, as if from the dead, wanting to talk to her? The very idea was so staggering Stella could hardly fathom it.

She'd known moments of anger in her life, but no amount of pain compared to the violence of her emotions against Ari's father, the man who'd come close to destroying her.

For him to think for one second she would pick up the phone and call him was too ludicrous to comprehend. The night she'd told him she was pregnant, he'd acted thrilled and told her he would find a way to take care of her and their baby. They would get married immediately despite their families being against it.

They had arranged to meet at the church, and once Theo arrived they would get married in secret, but Theo never came and Stella never saw him again. It was as if he'd simply disappeared off the face of the earth. The pain and the shame of waiting for him pretty well shattered her. Without Stasio's love and support, and of course the love she had for her gorgeous Ari, she probably would have died.

"I'm all right, Iola," she assured her. Sheer negative

adrenaline flowed through her body, driving her to get to her feet. She clung to the chair back while she waited for her head to stop reeling.

"Drink this." Iola handed her a glass of water.

It tasted good and she drank the whole thing. "Thank you."

"Theo Pantheras has obviously been stalking you. That is not good. You must call Stasio at once."

"No," she countered in a quiet voice. "That's the one thing I won't do. I have Ari to think about. This is something I intend to handle myself."

Since her parents' deaths, Stella had relied on her brother for everything. It had almost ruined his life in the process, but she wasn't a helpless teenager anymore. She'd grown into a twenty-four-year-old woman with a responsible position in the company, who'd been raising her son for the last six years.

Stasio had done more for her and her son than any human could expect of another. Her love for her brother bordered on worship. The only way to repay him in some small way was to leave him out of this. He had a wife and children he doted on, and Rachel was expecting for a third time. Stella wasn't about to impose her problems on him or his family. Never again.

She stared at Iola. "Not one word of this to anyone, especially not Nikos or Stasio. It will be our secret. You understand?"

The older woman nodded, but she said another prayer under her breath.

With no time to lose, Stella went upstairs for her purse. While there she phoned Dax's mother and told her she was coming to collect Ari. After telling Iola where she was going, she put the letter in her purse, then left the villa and drove to Dax's house.

As soon as Ari saw her, he ran down the steps of the front porch carrying his backpack and got into the car. She gave him a kiss on the cheek. "How was your last day of school?"

"Okay. We had to bring all our pictures and stuff home. Can we fly to Palaiopolis tonight?" It was the village on Andros where Stasio lived.

"No, honey. I'm planning to drive us tomorrow morning. I'd like my own car while we're on vacation."

"Hooray! I love our new car."

She chuckled. "So do I."

"Stasi says I'll be able to drive a car like this one day."

"Not for years yet, honey."

Whatever Stasio said, that was it. Long ago, when Stasio had told Stella he'd help her raise Ari, Nikos had warned Stella that Ari would always look to Stasio as his father. No other man could hope to compete. Nikos had told Stella that she should put her son up for adoption so he could have a normal life with a mother and father, but Stella wouldn't hear of it. Ari was her life! Since Theo had opted out of all responsibility, a boy could pray to have a surrogate father like Stasio.

While they waited for an old man to cross the street in front of them she glanced at her son. For six years she'd purposely concentrated on his Athas traits, but since receiving the letter from Theo, she was forced to take a second look at him.

Like Stasio, Ari was tall for his age with brown-black hair. He had Nikos's beautiful olive skin and her smile. But if she were honest with herself, his jet-black eyes, the musculature of his lean body, the shape of his hairline with its widow's peak belonged to Theo.

Pain stabbed her heart. Ari was the most adorable six-year-old in the entire world. Theo had no idea what he'd given up when he'd turned his back on the two of them. Why in heaven's name would he be interested in his child now? It didn't make sense.

She moved on. The breeze played with Ari's overly long hair. It had a tendency to curl at the tips, like Theo's…. Sometimes he held his head at an angle while he was looking at something with intensity, and again he reminded her of the man she'd once loved so completely she'd thought she couldn't live without him.

But that man who'd shown her so much love and had made her feel immortal had disappeared from her life. After realizing he was never coming back, she'd thought she was in the middle of a nightmare and would wake up. To her horror, she discovered she'd been awake the whole time. Welcome to the new reality of her life.

Remembered pain still had the power to shake her. She glanced at Ari. "Are you hungry?"

"No. Dax's mom fed us. Do you think Dax could come to Andros for part of our vacation?"

Any other time she would have said yes without thinking about it, but her entire world had been turned upside down this afternoon. She dreaded broaching the subject of his father with Ari, but if she put it off she would become more frantic than she already was. Then he'd know something was terribly wrong.

Ari had a very intuitive nature. Since she'd always been honest with him, she couldn't be any different now. When they pulled around the back of the villa, she didn't immediately get out of the car.

"Ari—before we go inside, there's something I have to tell you."

He looked upset. "Is it about Dax? You don't like him, huh."

She blinked. "Where did you ever get that idea? He's my favorite friend of yours."

"Because you wouldn't let him come with us to Andros last year, either."

Stella let out an anxious sigh. "That wasn't the reason. Dax's parents had other plans for him, remember? They took him to Disneyland. It was a surprise. That's why he couldn't come with us."

"Then how come you haven't said he can come with us this time?" He continued to look at her with those penetrating black eyes while he waited for an answer. Sometimes he could be very adult for his age. It always caught her off guard, probably because he reminded her of the Theo she had once known.

At sixteen Stella had been so shy and unsure of herself, yet he'd been tender and patient with her and he'd slowly built her confidence. When Nikos had been mean to her and made fun of her and her friends, Stella had turned to Theo, whose love and acceptance had made all the hurts go away.

Where had that man gone? After he'd disappeared from her life, she'd wanted to die.

Clearing her throat she turned to Ari and said, "Do you remember when you asked me if I knew where your father lived and I said no?"

All of a sudden she felt Ari go quiet. He nodded.

"It was the truth. I didn't know anything about him. When I asked why you wanted to know, you said there was no reason, but I knew that wasn't true."

He didn't move a muscle.

"I…I'm afraid I haven't made it easy for you to talk about your father," she stammered.

"Stasi said he hurt you so much you got sick."

"He was right. You see, my mommy died before you were born. Then your father went away and I never saw him again. I was so sad I fell apart for a while."

To make the pain even more unbearable, Nikos had been cruel and impossible to live with back then, always siding with their father that Theo came from the wrong kind of people with no background or class and no money. A marriage between them was unthinkable. She should be thankful he was out of her life.

Sensing how traumatic the situation was, how fragile her feelings were, Stasio had taken Stella to New York to have her baby. Six months later their father had suffered a fatal heart attack. After his funeral she and Ari had stayed in New York for the next four years. With Stasio there doing business half of every month, it had worked out well for all of them, and Stella had been able to get her college degree.

Thankfully at the time, Nikos went back and forth from Athens to the family's condo in Chamonix where he skied. She rarely saw him. That was a plus.

"Because of your uncle Stasio's love and kindness, I got better. The point is, that was a long time ago and a lot has changed since then." She moistened her lips nervously. "I found out this afternoon that your father has been living in New York."

His eyes rounded. "Just like *we* did?"

"Yes." That had come as another shock. For four years they'd both lived in the same city and hadn't even known it. Incredible. "However, he's back in Athens now to stay. He…wants to see you."

A long silence ensued. She could see him digesting what she'd just told him, but before he could ask another question, she needed to tell him the rest.

"Because it's been six years and he's never come near us until now, I need to know how you feel about seeing him. You don't have to answer right now. Just think about it. If you decide you'd like to meet him, then we'll call him up, but if you don't feel comfortable, Ari, you just have to say so—okay?"

If he didn't want to meet his father, then Stella would phone him when Ari wasn't aware of it. How she would love to hear Theo's reason for wanting to be with his child after all this time!

She couldn't imagine what Theo could say that would absolve him of what he'd done to her—to them! Stella couldn't comprehend a man walking away like that with no conscience, but it happened to other women all the time.

There were a lot of amoral men in the world, but she didn't want this one to be anywhere near her son. To her horror, Theo had brought up the possibility of getting the court involved if she didn't cooperate. She couldn't bear the thought of it, so she didn't dare ignore his letter.

Ari lowered his head. "I don't want to go and live with my father. I want to stay home with you. But I'd like to see him." He reached for her.

Waves of intense love for her son swept over her. "If that's your decision, then we'll tell him together."

He squinted up at her. "Can he make me go with him? Alex always has to go with his father to his new house and he doesn't like it."

Alex was one of Ari's friends. The situation in their home was very sad since his parents had divorced.

Her heart pounded with sickening intensity. The court could order visitation, but in the letter Theo had said he didn't want to go that route. Right now she was praying he meant it. "Let's not worry about that today."

In an abrupt motion Ari broke away from her and got out of the car with his backpack. "I'm going to call Stasi."

"No, Ari!"

That brought her son to a halt. He turned around, not quite believing her firmness. "Why can't I?"

"Because he's been forced to worry about us for too long as it is."

"But—"

"I said no." She cut him off before getting out of the car herself. "This isn't his business and doesn't involve anyone but you and me. Do you understand? After we go into the house we'll phone Dax's parents. Maybe they'll let him come to Andros with us for a few days. But whatever happens, when we get to the island, I don't want you to say a word about your father to anyone.

"Except for Iola, no one else knows he's back in Greece. You're not to tell the girls or Rachel or Stasio or Nikos. Can you promise me you'll keep quiet about it?"

"Yes." She'd thought the mention of Dax joining them might take the edge off this new worry in his life, but she was a fool to think that. After hearing his father wanted to see him, what little boy could think about anything else?

At this point Ari was horribly confused. So was she, and heartsick for him. His dark eyes filled with tears before he trudged toward the porch, leaving her devastated.

\* \* \*

The resort Theo had built on St. Thomas in the Saronic Islands brought an influx of the elite from the major continents. The manager Theo hired said they were fast becoming the preferred vacation destination in all Greece and had the statistics to back it up.

That was always good news, but after leaving Athens to spend the night here, he'd had other things on his mind. He'd give Stella another hour to respond to his letter before phoning her. There was no telling where she was right now. Probably with her brothers while they planned a way to stop Theo cold. It would do them no good.

There was a reason for that and it lay in front of him. The velvety green of the golf course extending in two directions from the sprawling white hotel represented many lucrative investments that now ensured Theo's wealth. It took this kind of money to be on a par with the Athas dynasty.

Theo had never been a mercenary man. He still wasn't. That was why the medium-size villa he'd had built on Salamis was comfortable without overwhelming Theo's own parents and siblings with a lifestyle foreign to them.

Needing an outlet for his energy, he walked around the resort to the marina. Most of the motorboats and small sailboats were out enjoying the beautiful late afternoon. One morning soon he'd take his boy out on the calm water.

He didn't doubt his son had been exposed to every water sport imaginable, but he'd only been taught by the Athas family. There was a whole side to him he didn't know about yet that only Theo could show him because he was his father.

After chatting with a few of the employees, he

entered the hotel and headed for the manager's office. The other man had arranged for Theo to meet the new head chef and go over the various menus for Theo's approval.

Once their business was concluded, he had the office to himself. Boris, his bodyguard, stood outside the room while Theo walked over to the window that looked out on the blue sea. He pressed the digit for Stella's cell phone he'd programmed into his. Nestor Georgeles, his attorney, had his methods of obtaining information. Theo flicked on the device that blocked his caller ID.

When Stella picked up after four rings, she was still talking to someone else. He could hear another voice in the background.

"Hello?"

It was her voice. Yet it was different. It was the voice of a woman.

"*Kalispera,* Stella."

He heard her sudden intake of breath. "Theo— h-how did you—" She paused. "Never mind. I guess I shouldn't be surprised."

"I have to admit that when I drove past your villa for old-time's sake, *I* was surprised to discover you hadn't aborted our baby after all."

"Aborted?" she cried.

Just then Stella had sounded too aghast at his comment to have faked it. He clutched his phone tighter. Among Nikos Athas's many sins, he'd coldbloodedly lied to Theo about Stella getting rid of the baby.

Sickened by the possibility that she'd really gone through with it and couldn't face him with the truth, Theo had left for New York determined to start a new life and make the kind of money so his family would never know poverty again.

However, now that he was back home and had discovered he had a son, no power was going to keep Theo from him. If Nikos interfered again and tried to do his worst, it wouldn't get him or her brother Stasio anywhere. Theo was more than prepared to fight fire with fire because he intended to be a full-time father to his child.

All these years he'd accused her in his heart of doing the worst thing a mother could do. He should have known she wouldn't have done away with their child. It wasn't in her nature. But for her to keep all knowledge of their son from him wounded him so deeply, he could hardly talk. His eyes smarted.

"What did you name him?"

There was a period of silence before she said, "I...I'm surprised you didn't find that out since you seem to know everything else." After another pause while he waited, she added, "He was christened Ari."

He sucked in his breath. "Is that an Athas family name?"

"No. I just liked it," she murmured.

Now that he knew that, he liked it, too. Very much, in fact. For the moment she was sounding like the old Stella.

In the past they'd been forced to speak quietly over the phone so her family wouldn't know she was making plans with him. She hadn't been allowed to start dating until she was eighteen, but she'd caught his eye before her seventeenth birthday. The thrill of falling in love had made both of them careless.

They'd slipped out at different times to be together. Theo had paid an old fisherman on a regular basis for the use of his wooden rowboat. There had been a protected cove on Salamis and he had always taken her there. They'd swim and then lie on a quilt spread on the sand. Theo knew he shouldn't touch her, but he couldn't help it, not when she begged him to make love to her.

She had been so giving, so utterly sweet and passionate while at the same time being so innocent, he had told her that if they waited until she turned eighteen, they'd get married and have a real church wedding. Though they'd tried to wait, there came a day when neither of them could stand it any longer. Once they'd made love, there was no going back.

He cleared his throat, intent on learning everything about his son. There were six years to catch up on. "If you could tell me the most important thing about him, what would it be?"

"I couldn't pick just one thing." Her voice shook. "He's sweet, loving. I think he's the smartest, kindest little boy in the world."

That described the woman he'd once loved. She'd spoken like a mother who adored her son. Ari sounded the antithesis of his uncle Nikos who years before had caught up to Theo with his first volley of threats. "Stay away from my sister or you'll live to regret it."

Nikos had been watching them at church, following them while they went for walks. When his threats didn't work, he had tried to bribe Theo with money. Theo had thrown it back in his face.

A week later there had been a small fire at his parents' taverna. The police had said it was arson, but they never found the perpetrator. Someone working for Nikos had phoned with more threats, and Theo had been warned there was more to come if he didn't leave Stella alone.

When Theo's brother Spiro had been injured on his

motor scooter by a luxury car driving way too fast for that time of night, Theo realized Nikos was in dead earnest.

The last time he ever saw Stella, she had told him she was pregnant. The news had overjoyed him and suddenly everything made sense. She'd been impregnated by a Pantheras. It was no wonder Nikos had behaved like a madman—Theo had violated his sister and there'd be hell to pay.

That night Theo had told her he wanted to marry her as soon as possible. They would go away and he'd get a good job to support her and the baby. They'd planned everything out and had decided to meet at the church in secret. But on the night in question, Nikos had been waiting for him in the church parking lot. He had told Theo that Stella wouldn't be coming now or ever, that she had aborted their baby and wanted to forget all about Theo.

In shock Theo had lunged for him, but he had been beaten up by hired thugs and left for dead on the island of Salamis. After he had recovered from his injuries he'd looked everywhere for Stella, but no one had seen her. She didn't answer his calls or letters. She'd simply vanished.

Eventually he came to the conclusion that she really didn't want to see him again. It was evident her family had talked her into getting rid of the baby. *His* baby.

He shifted his weight. "I've been waiting all day for your call so we could discuss Ari. When I didn't hear from you, I decided to phone you. Where and how would you like my first meeting with him to take place?"

"I'd rather it never happened in this lifetime or the next."

A nerve throbbed at the corner of his mouth. "Then you're saying you want this handled through the court?"

"No," she blurted in agony. For a moment she reminded him of the vulnerable girl he had once known. "I have to know what you plan to do. Ari keeps a lot of things to himself. Naturally he's frightened about things."

"So am I," his voice grated. "Do you have a sense of how he truly feels?"

A groan escaped her throat. "I wish I could tell you he despises the idea of you and would prefer you didn't exist, but the truth is, I have no idea how he feels deep inside."

In other words, Ari knew his mother hated Theo.

"Today he was probably reacting the way he did to please me. He always tries to please," she explained. "Maybe more than is healthy at times."

He had little doubt that Ari hated the man who'd fathered him and then had promptly rejected him even before he was born. A six-year-old could hate just as vehemently as a fifty- or an eighty year-old. Theo was under no illusion that this would be easy. In this case the hatred would be worse because Ari would have been indoctrinated by his uncles who'd wished Theo dead long ago.

He realized he needed to be prepared for hostility from Ari that might last a lifetime. A lot of factors would enter in, beginning with the atmosphere in which Ari had been raised, the amount of hate built up against Theo on the part of Stella's family. Her parents had been against him from the beginning.

Taking into account that the Athas brothers considered Theo the underbelly of Greek society and had done everything short of killing him to keep him away from Stella, Theo was starting off with an enormous minus handicap.

"Thank you for that much honesty, Stella." He hadn't expected it. "Since I already love him more than life itself and know you do, too, let's meet somewhere this evening to discuss him. A public place or not, whatever you prefer. Can you arrange for someone to watch him while we're together?"

"Of course, but it's not possible. I'm on Andros right now."

In other words, she assumed he was in Athens and that any plans he had for tonight were out of the question. He had news for her. "I can be there in an hour. Just tell me where you'll be exactly."

He counted a full minute while she was forced to realize he had a helicopter at his disposal. That put him in the same league with the way her family moved around. "There's a paddleboat concession on the beach in Batsi. I'll wait for you there in the parking lot at seven-thirty."

She clicked off before he could say thank you, but it didn't matter. Progress had been made. The gods had been with him today.

He checked his watch. It was six-thirty. After phoning the pilot to give him their next destination, he rang the manager to say goodbye, then headed for the helipad with Boris.

Theo had never been to Andros, but Stella had told him so much about it, he felt like he knew its special places by heart. Certainly his son, young as he was, could probably show Theo around and know what he was talking about.

Andros was the home of the legendary Stasio Athas, where some of the most elite Greek families lived. To the people in Theo's family it represented lala land. A smile broke one corner of his mouth. This Pantheras member was about to trespass on ground not meant for untouchables.

Stella's elite family viewed other families like Theo's, who lived close to the poverty line, at the bottom of the food chain. When Theo had refused the money Nikos had thrust at him to stay away from Stella, Nikos had snarled words like *scum* and *untouchable* among the many insults hurled at him. Nice people, Stella's family.

He looked out the window. Summer had come to the Cyclades. As Andros came into view, his breath caught at the lush green island dotted with flowers. No wonder Stella loved it here. St. Thomas was idyllic, but it didn't compare in the same way.

After the helicopter had dropped down over the little port of Batsi, his gaze swerved to a white convertible sports car driving along the road at a clip toward the water. The sight intrigued him. Once the chopper touched ground, he jumped down and started across the wooded area to the car park where it had just pulled to a stop.

To his surprise he saw a well-endowed brunette woman climb out and walk around the area with confidence, as if she were searching for someone. Closer now, he noticed she bore a superficial resemblance to the lovely long-haired teen of Theo's youth.

Stella.

# CHAPTER TWO

THE years had turned the only Athas daughter into a gorgeous female, whose classic white dress was cinched with a wide belt, highlighting curves above and below her slender waist. She'd always been beautiful to Theo, but having the baby had caused her to blossom.

Her high cheekbones, combined with the lovely contours of her face and glossy hair made her so striking, he couldn't look anywhere else.

He'd wondered how much she might have changed. What he hadn't expected was to feel his senses ignite by simply looking at her again. That wasn't supposed to happen, not when she'd kept all knowledge of their child from him.

Another step and their eyes met. Those velvety brown eyes he remembered so well stared at him with a mixture of shock and anxiety. After what she'd done, she ought to be terrified of him. She seemed to weave for a minute before she wandered back to her car and held on to the frame as if needing support.

He strolled up to the other side of the car. Deciding they were too much of a target for any observers, he climbed in the passenger side and shut the door. She hesitated before following suit.

The second she sat behind the wheel, her fragrance reached out to him. Again he was stunned because it was the scent he would always associate with her. It took him back to the last time they were together. Everywhere he'd kissed her, she'd tasted delightful, like fresh flowers on a warm spring morning.

Right now it was the last thing he wanted to be reminded of, but trying to blot out certain intimate thoughts was like attempting to hold back a tidal wave.

He turned to her, sliding his arm across part of the seat. She'd averted her eyes. If he wasn't mistaken, she was trembling. On some level it pleased him she wasn't in total control.

"Thank you for meeting me, Stella."

"You didn't leave me a choice." Her words came out jerkily.

"Actually, I did."

"You're talking about court. I can't imagine anything more terrifying for Ari," she cried, sounding desperate.

"Believe it or not, it frightens me even more. Too much time has been lost as it is." It surprised him how much he wanted to reach out and touch her, to see if she was real. "You were always lovely before, but you've turned into a startlingly beautiful woman."

If anything, her features hardened at the compliment.

His gaze drifted beyond her face. "Strange how this little secluded stretch of beach reminds me of—"

"Don't." Her profile looked chiseled. Apparently she'd had the same impression and didn't want to travel down that road of remembered ecstasy. "I agreed to meet you so we could talk about the best way to help Ari deal with this situation."

A situation that had been put in play six years ago

and was never of his choosing, but he didn't voice his thoughts. For the moment Theo was walking on egg-shells. "Do you think he'd be more comfortable meeting in Athens than here?"

She kneaded her hands, drawing his attention to her beautifully manicured nails. He grimaced to realize every part of her body looked quite perfect to him. It was impossible to eye her dispassionately. "Ari won't be comfortable anywhere with you, but since we're staying on Andros for a while, it should probably take place here."

"What have you told him about me?"

She sucked in her breath. "Very little."

"Even so, could you spell that out for me?"

Suddenly she jerked her head in his direction. Those gorgeous brown eyes pierced his with laserlike intensity. "You mean the way you spelled it out for me?" she cried. Her hands had gripped the steering wheel with enough force he imagined she could bend it. "I told him the truth, that you didn't love me after all, so we never saw each other again. That was all I knew to tell him. It's all he knows."

Theo studied her features. "Yet you left out half the story. It's time he heard that *you* stopped loving me. I'm sure he has no idea that you never intended to come to the church and go away with me so we could be married and have our baby in peace."

The blood seemed to drain out of her face. "I was there, waiting inside the back of the nave. I waited for hours," her voice throbbed.

Theo was incredulous. "That's an interesting fairy tale. I was attacked before I could make it inside and was told that you got rid of our baby because you didn't want anything to do with me." For now he didn't want to mention Nikos's name and give her something else to fight him about.

"You're lying!" she lashed out. "No one would believe such a monstrous story."

"In the beginning I didn't, either, not until you never, ever tried to make contact with me again. Obviously, this is a case of your word against mine, except I have the scars to prove it."

"What scars?"

"The ones you're looking at. While we've been talking, I've felt your eyes on me. They're traveling over the small cuts, noticing the dents where my face got smashed in and my nose had to be rebuilt. These are nothing compared to what my X-rays show below the neck."

Stella quickly concealed her glance, but not before he glimpsed confusion in those dark brown depths. That was something, at least.

"Whatever happened to you," she finally said in a less-than-assured voice, "don't you think it's stretching it just a little to take six years before showing up?"

"Under ordinary circumstances, yes, but after you were nowhere to be found and all my mail to you came back unopened, I realized I would have to return to Greece and hire a PI to locate you. Unfortunately, I didn't have that luxury at the time, not when I was building a business I couldn't leave."

Her head whipped around. "I don't know what mail you're talking about."

Theo reached in his trouser pocket for the first letter he'd sent to her after he'd gotten out of the hospital. He'd addressed it to Stella at the Athens villa. It had the canceled stamp and date. Across the bottom the words "Addressee Unknown" had been scrawled.

"Take a look." He handed it to her. "If you're ever curious enough to read what's on the inside of the envelope, then you'll know my state of mind at the time. In the meantime, I'm here to claim what's mine—Ari."

She glanced at the front of it before tossing the letter back at him. "Ari's not yours," she said in an icy voice he didn't recognize.

He put the letter back in his pocket. "Let me phrase that a better way. He's both of ours."

She threw her head back, causing those glistening dark strands to splay across her jaw. Combined with her golden skin, she was a miracle of womanhood. "You gave him life, but that's all you did."

"That was all I was allowed to do," he countered. "Since you clearly don't believe me, let's not talk about the past. It's over and done with. I much prefer to discuss Ari's future. Perhaps you could bring him here tomorrow so we can get acquainted. We'll let him choose what he'd like, or not like, to do. How does that sound?"

Her body stirred in agitation. "You can't expect too much, if anything, Theo."

As if he didn't know. "I'm aware of that. What time shall I meet you both?"

She started the car. "Tomorrow's Sunday. We have plans." She was stalling, but he had to be patient if he hoped to get anywhere with her. "The day after would be best. One o'clock."

"I'll be here. Stella, I swear I'll treat him with the greatest consideration possible. I'm not unaware he wouldn't be the marvelous boy he is if you weren't his mother. You were meant to be a mother, Stella. Every child should be so lucky."

Though they weren't touching, he could feel her

trembling. "Y-you can have two hours with him if he's willing," she stammered.

"That's more than I'd hoped for. The Stella I once knew was a giver. Remember that little heart I gave you?" It had been a cheap trinket he'd bought her in the Plaka because it had been all he could afford, but the sentiment had described her. "Love the giver."

She revved the engine, obviously not liking being reminded of anything to do with their past. "Please get out of the car. Ari's waiting for me."

There was a time when she would have begged him not to leave. Of course, back then he wouldn't have gone anywhere because he'd needed one more kiss, one more embrace before wrenching his mouth from hers. Damn if he didn't need her mouth so badly right now he was ready to explode.

Forcing himself to act, he got out of the front seat. "I love your car by the way. With its classic lines, it looks like you. In case you didn't know, that white dress was made for you."

For an answer she backed out and drove off.

Stella only made it two kilometers before she had to stop the car for a minute. She buried her face in her hands. How was it possible Theo could get under her skin like this after the pain she'd undergone at his hands?

Inside of half an hour he'd pushed every button until she'd wanted to scream. But what truly haunted her was the change in his facial features.

As far as the gradation of male beauty was concerned, Theo had been a beautiful man before. If she were honest with herself, he still was. However, one scar pulled at the corner of his mouth a little. His right eyelid didn't open as wide as the other. At some angles it gave him a slightly sinister look. His nose was still noble, but there were several bumps.

Theo hadn't lied about the damage done to him. As he got out of the car, she'd seen the scar below his left earlobe. A thin white line ran down his bronzed neck into the collar of his dark blue shirt.

The rest of his tall body covered by his elegant clothes revealed he'd grown into a powerfully built man. She didn't want to think about the damage beneath the surface he'd referred to, the kind an X-ray could detect.

He had an aura about him that hadn't been obvious six years ago, but that was because he'd needed time to mature. Other men would be intimidated by him now. She bit her lip because she recognized that women would be irresistibly drawn to him.

While deep in torturous thought, she heard his helicopter pass overhead. Embarrassed that he might think she'd had to pull over because of her reaction to him, she started driving through the cobblestone streets of Batsi toward Stasio's villa in Palaiopolis.

En route she picked up some toiletries in the village, proof of the reason she'd had to go out for a little while. She'd left the boys swimming in the pool with Rachel and the girls.

Unless Ari had let something slip to the family by mistake, she felt relatively confident they could keep Theo's presence a secret so they could get through this holiday without anyone being the wiser. On Monday she would tell the family she was going to drive the boys around the island as Dax hadn't been to Andros before.

Stasio worked so hard. Now that he'd taken three weeks off work to enjoy his wife and children, she didn't want her problems to mar their families' precious time together. Hopefully when Nikos arrived, he wouldn't cause trouble.

He'd been wildly against her keeping Ari. In his opinion it wasn't fair to their parents' wishes, nor to Stella, who didn't have a husband and who couldn't give Ari what adoptive parents could. He'd been furious at Stasio for helping her, telling him he should have kept out of things.

She knew Nikos didn't like Ari. Her son knew it, too, thus the reason he clung to Stasio who openly adored him. That Nikos couldn't show Ari affection caused Stella perpetual sadness and made it hard for her to be around him. A long time ago she had decided he didn't have the capacity to be happy, especially after their parents died.

Perhaps it was wicked of her, but a part of her hoped he might decide not to come this holiday. With the advent of Theo in their lives, Ari had enough going on without worrying about Nikos. But maybe she was getting way ahead of herself. It all had to do with Theo, who was well and truly back in Athens, demanding to spend time with her son.

His son, too, her conscience nagged.

No matter what terrible things had happened to Theo, surely it was too late for him to start up a relationship with Ari that should have begun at his birth?

Hot tears rolled down her cheeks. The agony of his rejection and the desolate years that followed could send her over the brink if she allowed herself to dwell on that nightmare. No more.

All she wanted was to be able to provide a wonderful life for Ari. She wasn't about to let Theo suddenly show up and turn their lives into chaos. Did he really think she would believe that the letter he'd shown her was authentic? She wiped the moisture from her cheeks before entering the gate that led up the drive to Stasio's villa.

Apparently she'd arrived in time to join everyone for a motorboat ride followed by dinner further up the coast. It was probably Stasio's idea because he knew Ari liked to steer part of the time, with Stasio's guidance of course. Undoubtedly Dax would get a turn, too. An evening out on the water sounded heavenly to her.

Stasio helped her into the boat with a hug. Her handsome brother looked so happy, she knew her secret was safe for the moment.

Theo flew to Andros on Monday at noon. He'd brought a backpack filled with treats and a few other essential items. Not sure what Ari would like to do, Theo had opted to wear casual trousers with a navy T-shirt and hiking boots. Today he would let Ari make all the decisions.

After grabbing a sandwich and a drink at a nearby taverna with Boris, he strolled over to the concession area to watch for Stella's car. It hardly seemed possible this day had come. He'd been dreaming of it for too long. This morning he'd awakened wired, unable to concentrate on his work.

The beach had filled up with tourists. He would have preferred not to be around a lot of people, but he had to follow Stella's lead if he wanted to gain a modicum of trust. While he tried to imagine his son's thoughts, his heart picked up speed as he spied Stella's car.

Riding with her were two boys of the same age sharing the passenger seat. One dark, the other blond, they pulled into the parking area. Stella had sprung a surprise on him. If she felt there was strength in numbers, that was all right with him. He'd deal with it.

Adjusting his pack to his shoulders, he approached the car. "Hello, Ari," he said, smiling at his son, who had on khaki shorts and a soccer jersey. He was on the lean side with black-brown hair; the kind of handsome child every man dreamed of fathering. The sight of him and his mother caused Theo's breath to catch in his throat.

He studied his son. The only thing that was going to guarantee any success at all was the purity of Ari's spirit and Theo's unqualified love for the child who was part him, part Stella. If their boy had inherited her sweetness, her loving nature, then maybe Theo had a prayer of getting through to him. But he knew it would have to be on Ari's timetable.

"Hi," he responded without enthusiasm, refusing to look at him.

"Who's your friend?"

"Dax."

"Hi, Dax. I'm glad you came. I want to get to know Ari's friends. I think there's a character on the *Star Trek* television series with your name? He has special powers."

Dax blinked. "I already know that. How did *you* know?"

"I love science fiction. Especially UFO stories."

"Me, too. My dad thinks they're stupid though."

"Well, I don't."

"Rachel knows some real ones," Ari said, drawn into their conversation in spite of himself.

"Who's Rachel?"

"My aunt. Her daddy was a pilot in the air force."

Theo's eyes took in Dax, who wore jeans and a tank top. Stella had put on trousers and a white blouse that her figure did wonders for. Considering everyone's attire to be appropriate, he made a decision.

"Your mother told me we would only have two hours today, Ari, but I think it's long enough to go for a hike. What do you say we all go?"

"That sounds cool," Dax responded enthusiastically.

Ari stared at Theo in surprise.

"You mean Mom, too?"

"She and I spent all our time outdoors. We must have walked all over Salamis Island. There's no one I'd rather trudge up a mountain with. In fact, I'd like to see if she can still keep up with me."

Theo moved around the other side of the car and opened the door for Stella, who looked at a total loss for words.

"I…I didn't plan to come with you." Her voice faltered.

"Please, Mom?" Apparently this idea pleased their son. With his mother along, he wouldn't be so afraid. Theo couldn't ask for more than that. She would have trouble refusing.

"I second the motion," Theo murmured. "You know all the secret places around here. I remember you telling me about the deserted lookout on the mountain behind us where you once found an eagle's nest."

Again Ari looked surprised. He stared at Stella. "I've never seen it."

"That's because I've never taken you hiking up there, honey."

Good. This would be a new experience for the four of them. "Let's find out if it's still there, shall we? I've brought enough goodies for all of us."

Everyone was looking at her. She could hardly say no. Stella would walk through fire to protect their son. "Well, all right."

While the boys got out, Theo assisted her. The sight of those long, elegant legs covered in khaki raised his blood pressure. When their arms brushed by accident, it sent a rush of desire through his body so intense he was staggered. To his chagrin, everything about her appealed to him more than ever.

"Ari? I bet you know how to put the top up on the car for your mother." The boy nodded, but Theo could tell Ari hadn't thought of it until it was mentioned. "That's good. We want it to be safe while we're gone. This car's a beauty," he said, eyeing Stella. She looked away.

"Will you let me do it, Mom?"

"I'll help," Dax volunteered.

"Yes. Of course." She'd been outvoted and outmaneuvered. Nothing could have pleased Theo more. He helped the boys and made easy work of it.

Once she'd locked the car with her remote, Theo opened his pack. "Give me your purse." Though he sensed she was fighting him every step of the way, she had to be careful in front of Ari. After she'd handed it to him, he zipped the compartment and eased it onto his shoulders a second time.

"If everyone's ready, there's a footpath beyond that copse of trees running up the side of the valley. Last one to the lookout is a girlie man."

Both boys laughed. Dax asked, "What's that?"

"A phrase I picked up while I was living in New York. It means wimp!"

Ari's smile faded. He stared hard at him as they walked. "Mom and I used to live in New York."

That was where she'd gone? Where she'd been for so long?

It was an astounding piece of news, despite the fact

that he knew Stasio did business there on a regular basis. To think Ari had been living in the same city where Theo had worked… So close? It slayed him. "Did you like it?"

"Yes, but I like Greece better."

"So do I."

"Come on, everyone," Stella urged. "At this pace we'll never get there." Theo wondered what had made her so nervous that she'd been a little short with Ari just now. A tight band constricted his breathing. By the end of their hike he intended to find out.

"I've never been to New York," Dax muttered.

"It's an exciting city."

"I thought you lived in Greece."

"I did until my twenties, Dax, then I moved to New York to earn my living. Now I have an office in Athens and am back to stay." Stella walked ahead of him with Ari, but he suspected she was listening to make sure the conversation didn't touch on things she wanted kept quiet.

"What do you do?"

"I deal in stocks and investments. Some real estate. What does your father do?"

"He owns a bank."

Of course. Dax belonged to the approved sector of Greek society. "Does your mother have a job, too?"

"No. She stays home with my brother and sister and me."

"You're very lucky. Do you know my mother still helps my father run their taverna on Salamis? I can't ever remember when they weren't working. Sometimes I wished my mother could stay home with me and my brothers, but we were too poor. She had to work."

"Is she a cook?"

Theo smiled. "She's a lot of things. The other day I

told her she and papa didn't have to work anymore because I planned to take care of them from now on. Do you know what she said?"

Dax looked up at him. "What?"

"'I've worked all my life, Theo Pantheras. If I didn't have work, I wouldn't know what to do with myself.'"

Ari slowed down and turned around. "Do they know about me?" Stella looked back. The pain in her eyes as she reached for their son tore him apart.

"They know all about you and hope the day will come when you might like to meet them."

To ease the moment, Theo pulled off his pack and opened a compartment. "Let's see. I've got water, oranges, peanuts, hard candy. Who wants what before we race the rest of the way?" The relief on Stella's face needed no explanation.

Once they'd refreshed themselves, Theo stood next to a pine tree. "I'm going to count to twenty while you two guys head up the trail first. Take my binoculars, Ari. If you see something exciting, shout."

The second he started counting in a loud voice, they took off on a run. It was steeper in this section and the trail zigzagged up through the forest. "Twenty!" he called out at last, then eyed Stella. "Are you ready to try catching up to them?"

"Just a minute, Theo."

"What's the matter? Are you about to tell me I've done everything wrong?"

Her chest heaved with the strength of her emotions. "Don't pretend you don't know you've done everything right," her voice shook. "Inviting Dax along made Ari feel comfortable."

"I thought that was why you brought him with Ari."

"No. I was going to take Dax on a little tour of the island while we waited for you, but your idea was much better." She wouldn't make eye contact with him.

"Then you're angry because I got you involved in the hike. When I saw Ari's face stripped of animation, I made an impulsive decision hoping it would help our son."

She wiped the palms of her hands against her womanly hips in a gesture of nervousness he'd seen many times years ago. He would always be touched by her vulnerability.

"Your instincts were dead on," she admitted. "I didn't expect him to have a good time today. Instead I…I have the feeling he won't be averse to seeing you again," she stammered. "That's what I need to talk to you about."

He chewed on some more peanuts. "Go on."

She cleared her throat. "We're here on vacation for two and a half more weeks." After a pause she leveled a guarded brown gaze with its hint of pleading on him. "Before you ask to see him again, would you wait until we're back in Athens?"

Two and half weeks sounded like a lifetime. "Of course I will," he answered in a husky tone without hesitation, "provided you tell me why you're so frightened for any more visits to take place here."

"I'm not frightened." Yet her whole trembling demeanor told him otherwise.

"Yes, you are." Without conscious thought he grasped her cold hands. "I take it your family is here and you haven't told them about me yet." Stella tried to pull away, but he drew her closer. "They're going to find out through Ari or Dax. You can't keep something of this magnitude a secret."

"Maybe not, but I'm hoping to deal with everything after we're back home in the city."

He grimaced. "It's like déjà vu, the two of us sneaking around to see each other without your family knowing what's going on. Nothing's changed has it."

"Please let me go." She tried to get away, but he still had questions.

"It wouldn't be because you're afraid to see me again, would it?"

"Theo—"

"Do my scars repel you so much?"

"Your scars have nothing to do with anything!" Her anger sounded genuine enough to satisfy him on that score.

"Then stay here with me for a little while."

"I can't!"

"That isn't what you used to say to me."

"You mean until you left me waiting at the church?"

"We've already been over this, Stella. I told you I came for you, but I was accosted. When I was able to search for you, you'd disappeared on *me*."

A strange cry escaped her throat.

His hands slid up her arms where he could feel the warmth of her skin through the thin material of her blouse, seducing him. He gave her a gentle shake. "Do you honestly believe I wouldn't have come to the church unless a life-and-death situation had prevented me? You and I talked marriage long before I found out I'd made you pregnant."

Her eyes filled with tears. "I don't want to talk about it. The boys might see us."

"They're at least a kilometer away by now. We *have* to discuss this at some point." He slowly relinquished his hold on her.

She shook her head, backing away from him as if the contact had been too much for her. "I don't know what to believe about anything. If you'll please give me my purse, I'm going back to the car while you join the boys."

He took several deep breaths to calm down while he got it out for her. The fact that she needed to run away from him meant it was possible his logic was getting through to her. His heart leaped. "Will you be all right going back alone?"

"That's an odd question to ask when you haven't been around in years. Please go and catch up to the boys. This is unfamiliar territory to them."

"I'll bring them back safely."

She darted away like a gazelle, leaving him bereft. He watched until he couldn't see her anymore, then he hurried up the mountain filled with new energy.

The Stella he'd loved to distraction was still there beneath her defenses, breathing life back into his psyche. He'd forgotten he could feel like this. In time he would get answers to why she never tried to get in touch with him again. She wasn't going anywhere now. Neither was he.

Before long he discovered the boys at the outlook. Dax had the binoculars trained on something. When he saw Theo, he pointed to an area along the ridge, then handed them over. Theo raised them to his eyes.

"You have a sharp eye, Dax. That's an Elenora falcon having fun with a friend."

They weren't thirty meters away. He handed the field glasses back. "Just like you and Ari."

Dax laughed, but there wasn't a glimmer of a smile from Ari's lips. Theo hadn't expected much positive reaction from his son yet and he wasn't getting it. To make progress he was going to have to practice infinite patience if he hoped Ari would let him into his life, let alone show him love.

Stella had received his promise that he wouldn't try to see Ari again until they were back in Athens. He had to honor it, but he didn't have to like it.

"I hate to break this up, but your mother is waiting for us." He opened his pack. "Finish off whatever's left and we'll go."

The boys needed no urging to eat the snacks. Theo packed the binoculars and they took off down the mountain.

Stella had already put the top back down. She looked as composed and untouched as before. Much to his satisfaction Theo could see the little nerve throbbing madly at the base of her throat, giving him irrefutable proof to the contrary.

When they reached the car, he checked his watch. The outing had taken three hours. More time with his son than he'd expected. He studied Stella's profile while he fastened the boys' seat belts and shut the door. "You guys were great sports today. I had one of the best times I've ever had. Maybe we can do it again some time."

Dax high-fived him. "It was awesome."

Ari squinted at him. "Is that your helicopter over there?"

His son didn't miss much. "Yes."

"Who's that man walking around?"

"My bodyguard. His name is Boris."

A short silence ensued. "Stasi has one, too." And his own hit men who included Nikos, but Ari wouldn't know that. "Are you going back to Athens now?"

Theo thought about his question. Ari probably

couldn't wait to get rid of him. But fool that Theo was, he'd dared hope he detected a forlorn tone in his son's question. Then again it was possible Ari was just being curious. Hell— Theo didn't know what to think.

Ari was his son, a boy he'd only known for three hours. The horror story of the past shouldn't have happened. His pain was starting all over again in a brand new way. "Actually I'm flying to my home on Salamis Island."

"Do you live with your mama and papa?" Ari asked quietly.

They are your grandparents, Ari. "No. They live in Paloukia, upstairs above the taverna." Ari wouldn't know what that would be like to live with so many bodies thrown together in a small space. So little privacy. The walls thin. Hand-me-down clothes. The smells from the kitchen permeating everything. "My house is on the beach about ten minutes away from them."

"Oh."

"Thank you for a fun hike, guys."

"It was cool!" Dax cried with enthusiasm. Nothing from Ari of course. Stella had averted her eyes.

Theo wheeled away from them and strode toward the helicopter. He didn't dare look back or he wouldn't want to leave.

# CHAPTER THREE

For one crazy minute a sense of loss swept over Stella, the kind she used to feel every time she had to leave Theo and hurry home.

No— This couldn't be starting all over again. She wouldn't allow it.

Like the other day she found herself speeding toward the villa while Theo's helicopter flew overhead. But there was one difference. This time she didn't stop to give in to her emotions or relive feeling Theo's hands on her again. Today he'd caught her off guard. Never again.

"When we get back and anyone asks, remember that we drove around, got some treats and stopped at Batsi to do some paddle boating. Do you guys think you can handle that?"

Dax nodded. Ari didn't say anything, but she knew he'd keep quiet. She wasn't surprised he was in a state of shock. A full dose of Theo Pantheras for three hours would awe any child, especially when the bigger-than-life man was his own father.

Once they reached the villa and the boys hurried to Ari's room to change into their swimsuits, Stella went straight to hers to call Dax's mom and assure her all was going well. This was the boy's first trip away from his parents with her and Ari. It was an experiment of sorts. So far Dax seemed perfectly happy. Theo had made the outing so exciting she doubted the boy had given home a thought.

She sat down on the side of her bed to phone her. As soon as they talked, maybe she'd be able to enjoy the holiday she'd been looking forward to before Theo had burst on the scene like one of those UFOs they'd talked about earlier.

That particular conversation had been a natural ice-breaker in ways Theo couldn't possibly have imagined. For his age Ari showed an interest in science fiction on an adult level. After the talks with his aunt Rachel, he was determined to be an astronomer when he grew up and search for new galaxies with life on them.

All this time Stella had thought he'd picked up this passion from his aunt, but now she was convinced he'd come by it through his Pantheras genes. Ari had several of the *Star Trek* series on DVD. Who could have guessed Theo was a *Star Trek* junkie too? It only showed Stella how little she knew about Theo.

"Stella?"

"Hi, Elani."

"How's it going with my boy?"

"They're having a terrific time. We just got back from a hike, and now they're going to swim."

"No problems yet?"

She smiled. "Not one." For the next few minutes she told her everything they'd been doing, only leaving out the details that Theo had been along. After Stella got back to Athens, she would confide in Elani about him. For now the episode on the mountainside when she'd been alone with Theo would be her secret. That was a mistake she wouldn't be making another time.

"Promise to let me know if there's any trouble with him and we'll come for him."

"So far so good, my friend. I'll make certain he calls you tonight before he goes to bed. I'm sure he'll want to."

"You're an angel, Stella. Talk to you later."

They both hung up.

Stella sat there in a daze, her thoughts on Theo. Though he might have killed her love long ago, the way he'd treated their son today convinced her he didn't want to make any mistakes with Ari.

She went over the day's events in her mind. He hadn't tried to influence Ari unduly or put fear in him with underlying threats of any kind. The truth was, he hadn't done one thing wrong. Not in front of their son.

The other part had been her fault for not telling Ari to go hiking alone with his father. Instead she'd let his apprehension persuade her to join all of them for the hike.

Except that wasn't the whole truth, and this was the part she hated admitting to herself. When Theo conned her into going with them, it hadn't been Ari she was thinking about.

Her curiosity over the man he'd become had been her Achilles' heel. In that moment of weakness she had given in and it had almost cost her her soul all over again. Would she never learn her lesson when it came to Theo?

She jumped up and hurried into the bathroom to put on her bathing suit. Amazing that on the way to meet Theo in Batsi, she'd imagined the outing would end in disaster, but nothing could have been further from the truth.

Stella was in shock. A new Theo had risen from the ashes, yet in all the ways that counted, she found him to be remarkably similar to the younger man. That Theo had stolen her heart before hurling it into the void where it could never be recovered.

Now he was back with a different explanation of what had happened the night she'd waited for him at the church. Wherever the truth lay, it had happened too long ago to do anything about now. The damage had been too pervasive for too many people. You couldn't go back and pick up the pieces. It wasn't possible.

"Mom?" Ari came running into her room.

"I'm in the bathroom changing!" Mortified that Theo was still on her mind, heat stormed her cheeks. "I'll be right there! I had to phone Dax's mother first."

"Aunt Rachel wants to know if you're coming out to the pool."

"Of course!"

"She says Stasi's starving and wants to eat outside now."

When her brother got hungry, it was wise to feed him. "Tell her I'll be right there," she called from the doorway. A second later she walked in the room with her towel and discovered Ari still standing there. Dax had to be downstairs. If Ari didn't want to talk, he would have run back to the pool.

"What is it, honey?"

He stared at her with the most somber expression. "Does my father want to see me again?"

Naturally it was about Theo. "You know he does. That's why he went to all the trouble to take you on a hike today."

"But he didn't say anything before he left in his helicopter, so does that mean he changed his mind about me?"

Was it fear or hope she heard in his question? "Ari, come here." She sat on the end of the bed. He walked over to her. "While we were alone, I told him our family is on vacation right now and asked him if he would wait to plan another visit until we get back to Athens. I hope that eases your mind a little."

By his frown, it appeared her answer didn't satisfy him. She began to realize there was nothing she could say to help him right now.

"Will I have to go with him?"

She sucked in her breath. "I tell you what. If you don't want to be alone with him, I'll go with you again next time." She searched his eyes. "He was nice to you today, wasn't he?" Her son didn't say anything. Stella couldn't tell what was going on in his mind.

Ari stared at his feet. She recognized that look of uncertainty. "Did your father frighten you today in some way I don't know about? You have to be honest and help me understand."

He shook his head. "No."

"But he did upset you, didn't he."

"Yes."

He dashed out of the room leaving her totally desolate. She hurried through the myriad of corridors and down some steps to catch up to him. When she reached the patio he was just jumping in the pool.

"Oh, good!" Rachel called to her. "Stasio! Come on out! We're ready to eat."

Stella found Dax and made sure he filled his plate. She fixed herself some food too and sat on the swing next to him because Ari was still swimming.

Speaking in a hushed tone she said, "Did you really have a good time today?"

He nodded. "It was great!"

"Then could you tell me what Ari's father did that seemed to upset Ari? Do you know anything?"

"No, but he got mad at me."

She frowned. "Mr. Pantheras got mad at you?"

"No. Ari."

"He did? When?"

"When we got back to the house he wouldn't talk to me and started playing with the girls."

That didn't sound like Ari. "I'm sorry, honey. His behavior doesn't have anything to do with you."

"He told me I should go home."

Stella hated hearing that. "He didn't mean it, Dax. Of course your feelings got hurt, but he'll get over what's wrong and apologize. After dinner I'll have a talk with him." *Another one.* "I bet he tells you he's sorry before we finish eating."

Except that Ari didn't do anything typical for him. He stayed in the pool, refused to eat and teased Cassie until she got out of the water and ran to her mother in tears. Even Stasio was aware something was wrong and got in the pool to talk to him.

But Ari wasn't having any of it and left the patio on a run. Stasio sent her a questioning glance. This wasn't good.

"Excuse me for a minute, Dax. I'll be back."

With a pounding heart she chased after her son. When she caught up to him, he was on the verge of locking his bedroom door.

"Ari—" She crushed him in her arms, refusing to let him go.

It didn't take long before the sobs came. In his whole life she'd never seen him convulsed like this.

"Tell me what you're feeling, darling. Let me help," she begged. "I know you're upset over your father."

"I don't want to talk about him."

"Then we won't."

"I'm glad I don't have to see him until after our vacation." He wiped his eyes. "I'm going to go back downstairs now."

"To talk to Stasio?"

"No."

"Then what?"

"Nothing."

"Please wait—" He was about to leave. "Dax said you got mad at him. How come?"

"Because he made me mad while we were hiking."

"I see." Except that she didn't. Dax was a darling boy. They'd always gotten along perfectly. "That happens with friends. You've had a lot of togetherness today. When you go back downstairs, do me a favor and make up with him? He's out on the patio feeling bad. If the shoe were on the other foot, you'd be feeling pretty awful about now."

"I don't want to make up."

"That doesn't sound like you." Stella didn't see her son act this way very often. "You still have to apologize because he's our guest. And while you're at it, how about telling Cassie you're sorry for keeping her beach ball away from her in the pool? She's only four, honey. When a big boy like you takes her stuff, she can't defend herself."

"Sorry."

"Tell *her* that. Okay?"

He nodded, then disappeared.

By the time she reached the patio, Ari had found Dax and had started to eat a lamb shishkabob with him while they talked privately. Pretty soon the boys got in the pool and played nicely with Cassie, letting her have the ball when it was her turn. Stasio flashed her a smile, glad all was well again.

Stella slipped in the deep end and did the backstroke, trying to unwind after a day she'd never forget. Ari might be acting normally right now, but she knew that deep inside, his emotions were in turmoil. So were hers.

Maybe she was wrong to ask Ari not to say anything to Stasio yet, but she wanted to believe they could handle this situation on their own. Stella hated to think she had such a weak character she always turned to her brother for help. How would Ari ever stand on his own two feet if he ran to Stasio every time there was a crisis? It had to stop.

The next day Stella walked into Ari's bedroom with some ice water for him. They'd just come back from a day's sailing. He'd picked up a little too much sun and complained he didn't feel very well. While the rest of the family and Dax played in the pool before dinner, she excused herself to see about him.

He lay on his back on top of the covers with his sun-tanned arm covering his eyes.

She sat down next to him and felt his forehead.

"You're hot. Drink this, honey. I'm going to get my phone and call the doctor."

She raced to her room, then hurried back to him. Relieved to see him drink part of it, she phoned information and got connected to the doctor's office. His receptionist said he was busy. After leaving a message for him to call, she hung up and took the glass from Ari.

"I don't want to see the doctor. I'll be okay."

"Let's let him be the judge of that."

"I wish Dax could go home, but I know he can't."

Dax again.

"Of course he can. All I have to do is call Elani and

she'll come for him." She studied him with an aching heart. He hadn't been the same since the hike with Theo yesterday. "Did you two have trouble again today?"

"Yes."

"Want to tell me about it?"

"No." He turned over so he wouldn't have to look at her.

"We have to talk, honey. Something's very wrong. Don't you know how much I love you?"

"Yes."

On impulse she said, "If you need to talk to your uncle about your father, then I'll ask him to come up here after he's through eating."

"I don't want Stasi." That had to be a first. He rolled off the bed so fast, she knew she'd touched a live wire.

"Why aren't you getting along with Dax?"

"Because he wants to talk about stuff I don't want to talk about."

"You mean like personal things?"

He nodded.

On a burst of inspiration she said, "Has he been asking questions about your father?"

"Yes."

"Like what?"

"He thinks my daddy is cool."

"I take it Dax got along well with him."

"They talked all the time."

She knew she was getting closer to some kind of answer. "Dax's father is an older man and fairly quiet. Dax probably liked Theo's attention."

"He keeps asking me about when I'm going to see him again so we can all do stuff together." His eyes filled with tears. "He's not Dax's daddy!"

"What do you mean?"

He blinked back the tears to keep them from falling. "My daddy liked Dax better than me."

*"What?"*

"I thought he wanted to be with me, but he was nicer to Dax. I hate both of them."

"Oh, darling!" Stella reached for him and hugged him harder while she tried to comprehend that far from feeling hostility toward his father, Ari was jealous of the attention Theo had paid to his best friend.

In order to feel jealous, it meant you had to care.

This meant Ari had nursed a longing for his birth father all his cognitive life, but it had lain dormant until put to the first test.

Before yesterday she'd assumed Theo would see that it was too late to bond with Ari. She'd been positive her son would never be able to warm up to him. Ari already had a surrogate father in Stasio, the best man in the world. He didn't need or want another one. In the end Theo would find out it was no use, but the surprise had been on Stella.

She had to do something immediately to help Ari, but what? Only one person had the power to make this right. For once it was beyond Stasio's ability to fix, which was a revelation in itself.

While she rocked her son back and forth, her cell phone rang. The last thing she wanted to do was answer it, but it was probably the doctor.

"Let me see who it is." She let go of him long enough to reach for her phone on the dresser.

She recognized the blank caller ID. It was Theo! She almost bit her lip all the way through before answering it. "Hello?"

"Stella?" The sound of his deep voice permeated

through her body to the soles of her feet. "I promised you I wouldn't try to see Ari until after your vacation, but I need to see you tonight. Alone," he added, sending a shock wave through her body. "I'm here in Palaiopolis at a small bistro called Yanni's. I'm seated at a table on the terrace overlooking the water and will wait an hour for you to come."

Stella's pulse sped up. She'd been there once with Rachel, but it was a romantic spot meant for couples so she had never gone to that particular restaurant again. "I-is there something wrong?" she stammered.

"Yes. I'll tell you when you get here."

She shifted her weight nervously. "I don't know if I can come without arousing suspicion."

"It's important." After a slight pause, "While you're thinking about it, I'd like to talk to Ari for a minute and tell him how much our outing meant to me yesterday. With Dax around I couldn't say all the things I wanted to. Do you think he'd be willing to come to the phone or call me back? If he doesn't want to do either, then I'll leave it alone."

Stella couldn't believe the timing of his call or the reasons for it. But she heard something in his voice that sounded like he was anxious. "Just a minute and I'll check."

She put it down on the dresser and walked over to Ari. "It's your father on the phone. He'd like to talk to you for a minute."

That brought Ari's head around. "What does he want?"

Her poor boy had been suffering all last night and today. She'd known it, but she hadn't known about the jealousy.

"He said there are things he wanted to tell you but couldn't because Dax was there. You don't have to talk to him now. He said you could call him anytime or not at all. It's your choice, honey."

He took a long time making up his mind before he walked over to pick it up.

She held her breath as he said a tentative hello.

At first it was a very one-sided conversation with Theo doing most of the talking. She thought it would end fast, but like every assumption she'd made since he'd come back into her life, he surprised her with the unexpected.

In a minute Ari grew more animated. He actually laughed at one point. Before the phone call, she hadn't thought it possible. The call went on another five minutes.

All of a sudden he said, "Mom?"

"Yes?"

"Do I have to wait till our vacation is over to see my father again?"

How utterly incredible! She'd died and come back to life several times since Theo had returned to Athens. "What about Dax?"

"Dad says I can ask him to come with us if I want. It's up to me."

Amazing. Theo had taken the sword out of their son's hand without knowing it. "Then it's fine."

Stella couldn't believe she'd just said that, but after Ari had been honest with her just now, she was thankful tonight's crisis had been abated by the only person who could help their son.

The fact that Theo was the cause of all the trouble in the first place hadn't escaped her, but none of that mattered in light of Ari's pain which seemed to have vanished at the sound of his father's voice. She would call the doctor back and tell him everything was okay after all.

"Mom? Do we have anything planned for tomorrow?"

That soon?

"Nothing special."

More conversation ensued before he walked over with her phone still in his hand. She waited for him to say something.

"Did you make plans?"

He made an affirmative sound in an offhand manner like it was no big deal, but the light in his brown eyes told her it was a very big deal.

"Mind filling me in first?"

"Dad's going to fly us to Meteora at four o'clock. He says that's where the monasteries are. We're going to hike around until it gets dark. He'll bring his telescope so we can look at the stars. Maybe we'll see some UFOs."

Stella could only marvel.

"It's a good thing your aunt Rachel won't know about this or she'd want to go with you."

"Don't worry. He said no women allowed this trip." This trip? Theo was doing everything right. She could find no fault. "I've got to tell Dax."

"Not yet," she cautioned him. "You and I still need to talk for a minute first. Stay here."

"Okay. Dad wants to speak to you again." He handed her the phone.

"Theo?" she asked too breathlessly for her own ears.

"Ari's response was more than I'd hoped for. It's yours I'm counting on now. This time, however, I'm the one waiting for *you* to show up. Let's pray no dark forces will prevent you from arriving."

Before she could say anything, Stella heard the click. It echoed the thud of her heart.

"Mom? Do you think Aunt Rachel would let me borrow her photos of Mars some time? I want him to see them."

"I'm sure she will."

"When do you think I could ask her?"

"Honey? I was hoping we'd keep this from the family until after we go back to Athens. You know, until we've got things a little more settled."

"Okay."

"Ari? Listen to me. Your father's here on Andros."

His eyes lit up. "He is?"

"Yes. He says he has to talk to me about something very important before he flies back to Salamis. I...I told him I would try to meet him, but I need your help because I don't want anyone else to know about it."

"I won't tell."

"I know that, so what I'd like you to do is stay here in your room and get ready for bed. I'll send Dax up to keep you company and you can tell him what your father has planned for tomorrow. In the meantime I'll tell Rachel I need to do an errand and will be right back."

"I wish I could go."

"Not this time, honey. Your father and I have things we need to discuss alone. Can you understand that?" He nodded. "You'll be seeing him tomorrow, right?"

His lips broke into a smile. "Yeah."

Stella kissed him and hurried to her room for her purse. She didn't dare change out of her pants and top she'd worn sailing. It might give her away.

"Rachel?" she said a minute later. Everyone was out by the pool eating. "Ari's resting. I think he got too hot, but he's feeling better now. Anyway, I'm running into town for some things he wants. I'll be back shortly." She turned to Dax. "When you're through eating, Ari hopes you'll come up."

"I'm all finished," he declared before darting away.

Glad everyone was preoccupied with the girls, Stella hurried out to her car and headed into town. On the way she phoned the doctor and told his receptionist that Ari was doing much better so the doctor didn't need to call back.

Due to the tourists, she had to park a street away from Yanni's. It was getting crowded. By the end of the evening, the night life would take over.

She hurried inside the bistro and told the hostess she was meeting someone out on the terrace. There was no sign of Boris, but that didn't mean he wasn't there.

The other woman showed her to Theo's candlelit table on the terrace. With every step, she wished she'd been able to wear an evening dress at least. Especially when she saw him get to his feet wearing an expensive black silk shirt and gray trousers. He stood out from the other males, drawing feminine attention from every direction including that of the sultry hostess.

His black gaze swept over Stella with that old intimacy. When he helped her to be seated, she felt his hands caress her shoulders lightly, as if he couldn't help himself. It took her back to another time when they hadn't been able to keep their hands off each other.

"You picked up a lot of sun today," he whispered against her ear. "Your beauty radiates like a torch. Every man out here envies me."

She tried not to react, but inside she was a quivering mass of emotions. Theo always did have that effect on her. Right now she was in danger of forgetting the chasm of pain separating them.

Once he was seated he said, "Since I knew you couldn't be gone long from the villa, I took the liberty of ordering for us."

Stella could hardly breathe for the way he was devouring her with his eyes. "You're very sure of me, aren't you."

His gaze narrowed on her features. "I'm sure of what we felt for each other before we were tragically prevented from getting married. Nothing since that time has changed for me. I'm operating on the belief that deep down you still have feelings for me."

She looked away while the waiter served them baked shrimp with garlic and onions. Theo remembered. It was one of their favorite dishes, accompanied by bread and a glass of house wine.

After their server had gone, she began to eat, realizing she was hungry. "This is delicious."

"Like the shrimp we used to eat at the Blue Lagoon during our walks on Salamis."

She reached quickly for the wine, wishing he wouldn't remind her. "We don't have much time. Why don't you tell me what's so important you had to see me tonight."

He broke his bread apart. "I asked you here to let you know I want a relationship with you, not just Ari."

The world reeled for a moment.

Theo had always been frank and direct. In that regard he hadn't changed, but life had changed the situation. She had to keep her head. "If you'll take a look around, Theo, there are any number of females who'd like to accommodate you given half a chance."

A sly smile broke one corner of his compelling mouth. "What females? I only see Stella Athas, the girl who ruined all other women for me."

"Theo…" her voice throbbed.

"You did, you know." He cocked his head. "I saw a lot of women in New York and found every single one wanting. I'd hoped to meet someone who would make me forget you, but it never happened. Believe me, if it had, I would have married her and stayed in the States."

His words sent a shiver through her body. After seeing him again, after knowing what he already meant to Ari, the thought of him married to anyone else brought a fierce new pain to her heart.

"How many men have you known since me?" His deep voice had taken on a territorial quality.

"That's none of your business."

"How many, Stella? They must be legion."

She stared at him through veiled eyes. "If you're asking what I think you're asking, the answer is none."

"But not for want of trying?" He lifted the last of the wine to his lips.

"I've been too busy raising Ari."

His jet-black gaze seemed to gleam in the flickering light. "You've done a superb job."

"Thank you." She couldn't handle this conversation any longer. After putting her napkin down, she got up from the table. He didn't make a move to stop her. "I have to buy a few items in town before I return to the villa. If I'm gone any longer, the family will wonder why."

"We can't have that, can we," he drawled.

Theo knew she was worried about her family's reaction to him being in her life again. It made her unable to sustain his glance. "I'll have the boys waiting at four."

"Come with us tomorrow."

"No," she blurted. She was in too deep already. Any more time spent in his company would confuse her even more. "Ari's looking forward to being alone with you. Good night, Theo."

After a few purchases she headed back to Stasio's. On her way, she needed to figure out an excuse why she and the boys would be gone from the villa tomorrow. She couldn't say they'd be going on a drive around the island again.

By afternoon of the next day Stella had finally come up with a plan. She told the family they'd decided to take a long hike in the mountains. Afterward they'd get a big dinner at one of the restaurants in Batsi and see a film, thus the reason they'd be home late.

At four, when she drove into the paddleboat parking area with the boys, Theo was waiting for them in thigh-molding jeans and a creamy cotton crew neck sweater. He looked so striking her pulse ticked right off the charts.

He put his hands on the door frame next to her. She felt his gaze wander over her, missing nothing. The smell of the soap he used had a familiar tang, causing her to tremble. "We'll be back at ten. Will you plan to join us for a light dinner afterward?"

"I don't think so." She looked at Ari who was still sitting next to her. "This is your night with your father."

"But I want you to come, Mom." He leaned closer and gave her a kiss on the cheek. On that note he got out of the car with Dax.

"You may be too tired to eat a meal that late. Why don't we see what happens."

"I'll take that as a yes" came Theo's low, smooth re-joinder before he put an arm around Ari's shoulders.

Stella didn't know her son, who laughed freely before the three of them hurried toward the waiting helicopter. She stared after them. Was that Theo's first physical gesture of affection toward their son? If so, Ari appeared to welcome it.

The two of them seemed to be bonding before her very eyes. If things continued like this, then she had to face the truth. Theo planned to be Ari's father in every sense of the word, something Ari obviously wanted. That meant Stella needed to grow another skin to survive.

Last night he'd told her he wanted them to have a relationship, but she was terrified. Right now the lines were blurred because she had an undeniable fatal attraction to him. Stella feared that given more time, she'd be right back where she'd started—madly in love with Theo.

On a groan, she walked toward the little town of Batsi where she would while away the hours until their return. She heard the helicopter pass overhead. The sound caused her to quicken her pace so she wouldn't think about the excitement she was missing by not being with them.

# CHAPTER FOUR

THAT night Theo took the hostess aside and slipped her a tip. "Can you put us in front where the boys can watch the dancing up close?" He'd picked a taverna in Batsi that was tourist friendly regardless of ages.

"If you and your wife will follow me, I'll seat you."

"Thank you."

Stella had to have heard what the other woman said, but she pretended not to notice. Ushering the boys forward they moved through the crowded terrace to a table overlooking the bay. How many years had he dreamed of being with Stella like this, knowing he could take care of her and his own….

Several couples were already on the dance floor moving to the live band. He was aching to get her out there. Once he got the boys started on some snacks, he planned to steal her away where they could keep an eye on them while he held her as close as decency allowed.

Once a waiter came for their orders and the boys had told Stella about their outing, he asked to be excused before grasping her hand.

"Dance with me?"

"Do it, Mommy. I've never seen you dance before."

"She's an expert," Theo murmured. Without waiting for a yes or a no, he drew her out of the chair onto the floor.

Her body was stiff. "I haven't danced in years."

"Neither have I. The last time was at a church dance with you. Do you remember it was in the basement? Everyone was afraid with all the adults watching. I stepped on your foot."

"No, you didn't. I was the one who stepped on yours several times. I was so embarrassed I wanted to die."

He caught her close, pressing his cheek against the hotness of hers. "All I remember was that I was in heaven because Stella Athas, the most desirable girl in the world, had agreed to dance with me. I was the envy of all my friends who laid bets you wouldn't let me get near enough to touch you."

"Was I that impossible?"

"I thought that at first, but soon discovered you were just painfully shy. You presented a challenge I couldn't resist. My biggest fear was that once you found out I was a Pantheras, you would run from me and go to a different church where I couldn't find you."

"When I was a teenager, the last thing I thought about was money."

"I know that now, but everyone whispered you were an Athas who couldn't see the urchins at your feet."

She pulled back, staring at him through wounded eyes. "How awful that people felt that way."

"Not everyone, Stella." Obeying an insatiable need, he brushed his mouth against hers before winding his fingers into the back of her hair. She was so beautiful. She could have no idea how much he'd missed feeling her next to him.

Her eyes closed tightly. "Please keep your distance. We're on a dance floor with the children watching."

Theo couldn't help smiling. "Everyone else is dancing close." He was fast losing control.

"We're not everyone."

"No, we're not, thank heaven. There's only one Stella." He kissed her hair at the temple. "There are things we have to talk about. Expect a call from me before you go to bed tonight." Theo swung her toward their table and held the chair for her to sit down.

"How's the food, guys?"

"Good," Ari said. "The waiter brought us more drinks."

Dax nodded. "He said we could have as many as we wanted."

Feeling euphoric, he eyed his son. "Have you ever danced with your mother before?" He shook his dark head. "Now's your chance."

"I don't know how."

"I do. My mom taught me." Dax got up and went over to Stella.

She smiled. "I'm honored." Without hesitation she took him for a whirl around the floor.

Theo grinned at Ari. "You see? There's nothing to it."

He could tell his son was girding up his courage. A minute later they came back to the table. To Theo's delight, Ari got up and took his turn with Stella. Nothing like a little healthy competition.

Good for him. He had a shy side like his mother. With a little confidence, he was going to grow up to be an outstanding man. Whatever he chose to do, be it astronomy or otherwise, he had the intelligence and perseverance to succeed. Theo wanted to be his father on a twenty-four-hour basis. The way to do that depended on getting through to Stella.

As if she knew what he was thinking, the minute she came back with Ari, she checked her watch. "It's really late. I'm afraid we have to be going."

Theo put some bills on the table and helped Stella to her feet. The four of them left the restaurant and walked out into the warm Greek night. He accompanied them to the car, knowing better than to hug her too tight.

This time he high-fived his son first. "I had one of the best times of my life today."

"Me, too."

"You can call me anytime. When you're back in Athens, check with your mother and we'll make more plans."

Ari's head whipped around to Stella. "Can't we decide now?"

She looked tormented. "We'll talk about this later."

"Your mother's right. It's been a long day." He tousled both boys' hair, then flicked her a glance. "Drive home safely. Your car holds precious cargo."

Their eyes held for an instant before a look of determination to leave altered her features and she started the car. Ari looked back while they drove away and waved.

He raised his hand. Keep it up, Ari. Keep it up.

No sooner did the three of them walk into the villa than Stella heard a voice that always made her uneasy call to her. It was terrible to feel that way about her own brother, but there'd been too much history in the past to pretend his presence didn't affect her.

"Well, well." He scrutinized the three of them. "Who would have imagined you keeping such late hours."

"Hi, Uncle Nikos."

She paused in the entrance hall to give him a kiss on the cheek. He looked lean and dashing in his swim trunks. Her brother was the personification of the Olympic silver medallist who'd won one of the few medals for Greece in the downhill and giant slalom. He was an icon in his own right.

"Hello, Nikos. It's good to see you. Where's Renate?"

"Upstairs unpacking." His glance alighted on Dax. "Who's this?"

"My friend, Dax."

"Haven't seen you around here before."

"Ari invited me."

Knowing Ari felt uncomfortable, Stella put a hand on their shoulders. "Hurry on upstairs and get ready for bed. Don't forget to brush your teeth. I'll be up in a few minutes to say good night."

She gave them each a kiss before sending them off. Without the boys around, it was easier to deal with Nikos. "Is Stasio still up?"

"They're out on the patio. Are you joining us?"

"Not tonight. To be honest, I'm exhausted. Tell Renate I'll see her in the morning."

"How come you let Ari bring someone? This is our family time."

Stella bristled. "I can't believe you just said that. He's not going to be here the whole time, but even if he were, what difference does it make to you? You'll come and go as the mood suits you. As for the girls, they're two and four, hardly company for a six year-old all the time."

He looked taken back. She couldn't remember the last time that had happened.

"Since when did you become so prickly? I hardly know you like this."

"I didn't pick this fight, Nikos. You did by being offensive, not only to me but the boys." Theo had shown more loving kindness to Dax than Nikos had ever shown to Ari.

"Stella?" he called her back, his dark eyes angry. "What's gotten into you?"

"I'm still the same person. I've just decided to speak my mind the way you do. Sometimes it's not pleasant is it? Good night."

She walked up the stairs without looking back. It had felt good to be honest with him. However, there was no deluding herself. For as long as he stayed on Andros with his Austrian skier wife, also an Olympian, Nikos would make her and Ari pay the price.

That was still on her mind when she reached her room and discovered her son waiting on the top of her bed in his pajamas. Somehow it didn't surprise her.

"Hey, honey...why the long face after such a wonderful outing?"

"Mom? Do we have to stay here for our whole vacation?"

*Thank you, Nikos!*

"It's what we'd planned."

"But I want to be with my daddy. He has all these fun things we can do at his house."

She'd thought this was about Nikos, but it clearly wasn't. Stella took a steadying breath. "Haven't you been enjoying it here?"

He averted his eyes. "Yes."

"But?"

"I like being with him. He's awesome. Dax says so, too."

"I noticed. Is it like being with Uncle Stasio?" He was Ari's hero.

"Kind of, but he's my papa," he said quietly.

His papa…

"I wish we could go home tomorrow."

Knowing he already felt this strongly about his father, she had no doubt this was going to be a permanent situation from now on. But she needed to know a lot more about Theo's agenda. He wouldn't always have this much free time to spend with Ari. Her greatest desire was to protect their son from being hurt.

The fear of history repeating itself was uppermost in her mind, especially when things were moving so fast. Their lives were changing in ways she hadn't thought possible a week ago. Certainly Ari's world had undergone a total transformation.

"Tell you what. Your father will be calling me in a little while and we'll talk. I'll let you know what we decide in the morning."

His crestfallen look spoke volumes. He wanted answers now, but she couldn't give him one. "Okay." He slid off the bed and darted out of her room.

Her mind on Theo, she went into the bathroom to brush her teeth. If he'd flown straight to Paloukia, then he was probably home by now. She decided to get ready for bed first. Maybe by then he would phone her.

Ten minutes later she slid under the covers, still waiting for his call. Deciding to take the initiative, she reached in her purse for his letter and dialed his cell phone number. He picked up on the second ring.

"Ari?" The tender excitement in his voice was a revelation in and of itself.

"No. It's Stella. Is it a bad time for you to talk?"

"It's a perfect time. I just walked into the house and was about to call you."

She'd thought she could do this, but now she wasn't so sure. Too nervous to lie there, she got out of bed and began pacing.

"This is about Ari."

"I presumed as much, but I live in hope the day will come when you and I can have a conversation about the future. Our future."

Her breath caught. "We don't have time to talk about that right now."

"Why not? Did Ari get sick on all those hors d'oeuvres they ate while we were dancing?'

"No." She wished it were that simple. "Since he's been with you, he's a different boy."

"So am I. That's what happens when a father and son get together."

"That's my concern." She crushed the phone in her hand. "For how long?"

"Forever."

Her body started to shake. "Lots of relationships start out on a forever basis, but deteriorate with time."

"Our love didn't die, Stella," he declared in his deep male voice. "We were ambushed by a force neither of us had the power to stop at the time."

"You keep saying that!" she cried.

"Because it's true. If I thought you would take me at my word that I was torn from you, I'd never tell you another thing because I don't want you and Ari to go through any more hurt."

"What hurt? After what happened, how could there possibly be any more? Look, Theo—for Ari's sake I want to believe you because he wants to be with you, but I'm afraid my ability to trust died years ago."

"So, what are you saying?" His voice sounded bleak.

"Th-that I'm going to go on sheer faith and give you free access to him." Tears rolled down her cheeks. "You've got Ari's heart in your hands. If you do anything to disappoint him…" She couldn't talk for a minute.

"I'm here to stay, Stella. My life is totally tied up in him."

This was hard. So hard when those were the things she'd wanted him to say to her years ago.

"I pray you're telling the truth, because tonight he asked if we could cut our vacation short and go back to Athens in the morning. He wants to be available to you."

"What did you tell him?"

"That we'd talk about it in the morning."

"I'm sure that's the last thing you want to do when you love being with your family. They still don't know I've been seeing Ari?"

"No. It's my business. I've preferred keeping things private. They'll find out soon enough. I'll be driving back home in the morning with the boys."

"In that case I'd like to come to see him tomorrow afternoon. The three of us can talk over plans then."

"He'll be thrilled," she murmured.

"Even with all our history, it'll be the first time for me to make it inside your home, Stella."

She realized that. Years ago they'd had to be careful when he brought her back from an outing on his brother's motor scooter. He'd leave her a block away, then wait for her call when he got back home to make sure she was all right. Theo had never failed her. That's why his unprecedented behavior on that horrific night had been too much for her psyche to handle.

"Ari will be overjoyed." But nothing else has been resolved.

"No more than I. Thank you. This means more than you will ever know." His voice sounded thick-toned.

*Get off the phone, Stella.* "Good night."

"Good night. Drive home safely." She heard the concern in his tone before hanging up. The rest of the night she tossed and turned, hoping she'd made the right decision.

The second Ari came in the next morning, she told him they were leaving. He whooped it up before running to tell Dax to get his stuff together.

Stella packed quickly before going down to Stasio's study. He usually checked in with his secretary in the early mornings, even when he was on vacation. Like Theo, he was tall with arresting male features. There wasn't a mean bone in his body.

"Knock, knock."

"Stella? We missed you last night. Come on in."

"I'm just peeking in to say goodbye for now. Let's hope Rachel's morning sickness improves."

He frowned. "Bad as it is, I'm more concerned about you at the moment. Tell me what's wrong."

"Nothing specific." She hated lying to him, but she wasn't ready to talk about Theo yet. "Ari and Dax are restless. At home they have more friends their own age to do things with."

He studied her through veiled eyes. "You're not telling the truth, but that's your privilege. I've seen a marked difference in both of you since you arrived. Just remember, I'm here if you need me."

Her brother had radar. "I've always known that and I love you for it. Tell Rachel I'll call her later today after I'm back at the house. Say goodbye to Nikos and Renate for me, too."

Stasio came around his desk and gave her a big hug. "I'll walk you to the car."

The boys were already strapped in. It was so unusual for Ari not to seek his uncle out first, Stasio had to know something of great significance was going on.

"See you later, Uncle Stasi. Thanks for a great time."

"I had fun, too. Thanks a lot," Dax said.

"You come again, anytime you like." He gave Ari a hug.

Stella started the car and they took off for the port of Gavrion to catch the ferry.

No sooner had they driven onboard and walked to the promenade deck than a steward approached Stella.

"You are Despinis Athas?"

"Yes?"

"Your room is ready for you."

She blinked. "I didn't reserve one." Depending on weather and wind conditions to Rafina, the cruise only took two to three hours.

He gave her a knowing smile. "Someone else did. This way please."

"Come on, boys. Someone has planned a surprise for us." The blood hammered in her ears. She could only think of one person.

They followed the steward down to the next deck. He led them around a passageway to a row of cabins and opened the third one for her. Stella gasped when she walked in and saw two dozen long-stemmed red roses in a vase on the nightstand between two double beds.

To one side was a table and chairs. She spied a bowl of fruit, another filled with candy and cookies, and half a dozen cans of various juices.

"Are these for *us?*" Ari cried in delight.

"Who else would they be for?" sounded a deep, familiar male voice.

Stella spun around. "Theo—"

"Papa!" Ari ran to hug him. "We didn't know you were coming with us!"

Theo's black eyes found Stella's. They were so alive she could feel his energy. "Work can wait. I decided I wanted to join in the fun."

"Goody!" their son cried while Dax beamed and began loading up on candy.

Stella was happier to see him than she'd thought possible. "The flowers are gorgeous."

He came all the way inside and shut the door before leaning against it with his arms folded. In a tan sport shirt and white shorts, he looked incredible. "Remember the time we took a ferry to Poros? It was so crowded we had to stand the whole way against the railing at the back? I only had one red rose to offer you. In those days I was so poor, I could only afford to give you token presents."

Stella cherished any little thing he ever did for her. "I still have it," she half whispered. "It's pressed in the big dictionary I keep on my bookshelf at home."

"I've seen that," Ari commented. "I didn't know Daddy gave it to you."

Theo's white smile turned her heart over. "Your mother and I liked to give each other little gifts. I still have the bracelet she once bought me."

Ari munched on a cookie. "Where is it now?"

"Right here." Theo lifted his leg. They all stared at the tiny gold chain around his ankle.

"You still wear it?" Stella was in shock.

"I told you that night I would never take it off."

Her face went hot. Before they'd gone swimming, she'd given it to him and he'd made her put it on him. She remembered him crushing her in his arms, telling her they were now joined forever.

"I want to get one."

"Me, too!" Dax chimed in.

Stella laughed. "Maybe when you two are older."

"Speaking of you two…" Theo walked over to the closet and pulled out a couple of junior life preservers. "I want you to put these on and wear them the whole time." He helped them get them on.

"How come?"

He finished tying them. "Because you never know when something could happen and I want you to be safe."

She could see Ari wasn't too happy about it, but she loved Theo for insisting.

"I bet nobody else is wearing one."

"Maybe not, but I want you to do this for me because I love you so much."

"I love you, too, Papa. Now you have to put yours on."

Both Stella and Theo burst into laughter. He pulled two adult jackets from the closet. "What's good for the goose, eh?" He started toward her with a wicked glint in those fabulous black eyes.

Stella would have put it on herself, but Theo insisted on doing the honors. His touch sent curls of delicious warmth through her body. With his back toward the boys, his eyes ignited as he took his time tying the ends near her throat. She wanted him to kiss her so badly she felt pain to the palms of her hands.

Needing something to do before she acted on her desire, she took the other life jacket and helped him put it on. Had he always been so broad-shouldered and powerful? When her hand touched his chest, she heard his sharp intake of breath.

"Can we go play shuffleboard?"

"Yes," Theo answered while she was still fastening his tie. "We'll come up and join you in a minute."

"Okay. Let's go, Dax!" They grabbed some candy and left the cabin.

When the door closed, Theo pulled her closer to him. "Our son just did us a favor. Without this body armor, you wouldn't be safe from me right now. Let's try it out, in case I'm wrong."

Before she knew what had happened, she was engulfed in his arms, unable to move. "I'm going to kiss you whether you want me to or not."

She thought he would start with her mouth, but he began an exploration of her face, slowly inching his way around until she thought she would die if he didn't satisfy the craving building inside her.

A moan escaped her throat, her body's way of begging him to stop torturing her and really kiss her. When it came, she almost fainted from ecstasy.

Somehow, she didn't really know how, they ended up on the bed in a kiss that seemed to have no beginning or end. She lost complete track of time. It was just the two of them communicating in a wine-dark rapture of need escalating out of control.

Suddenly the door opened. "Hey, Mom? Papa? Aren't you going to play with us?"

Theo recovered first. He bit her earlobe gently, then rolled off the bed. "I'm coming up now. Your mom will join us in a few minutes. You guys want some drinks?"

"Yeah. Thanks."

After they left, Stella sat up, but her head was so

woozy from being kissed senseless she had to maneuver carefully so she wouldn't fall over when she stood up. The life preserver made it difficult.

One look in the mirror over the dresser spoke a thousand words and needed no translation. It took her back to her teenage years. After being with Theo, her lips were always swollen, her face flushed and the hair he loved to play with was in disarray.

She buried her face in one of the roses. Their scent filled the room. Whenever she smelled roses in the future, she would remember this day and treasure it. Once again Theo had worked his magic.

After brushing her hair and putting on fresh lipstick, she phoned Elani and told her they were coming home but were still going to keep Dax if it was okay. With that accomplished, she went up on deck to find the guys.

They all played shuffleboard, then walked around to watch the water traffic. Theo entertained the boys. She mostly listened. Eventually they went back to their cabin for more treats. While the boys stretched out on one of the beds, Theo lay on his side behind Stella who sat on the edge of the bed to talk to them.

He did it on purpose, knowing it would be pure torture for her not to be able to lie down next to him. Ten minutes to port her cell phone rang. She checked the caller ID. It was Rachel. She had to answer and said hello.

"Stella—I had no idea you were going to leave today. Stasi let me sleep in. I just woke up and found out you'd gone. Cassie's so upset."

She got up and went outside the cabin so she could talk in private. "I'm sorry, Rachel. It's just that with school out, Ari and Dax want to do some things with their friends."

"I understand, but I have to admit I'm disappointed."

"Forgive us."

"Of course."

"We'll be back again after Dax goes home in a few days."

"I'm counting on it. Take care."

"You, too. I want you to get over your morning sickness."

"It'll pass. Talk to you later."

Stella hung up feeling horrible, but she couldn't change plans now. It was very evident Theo and Ari loved each other and wanted to be together. This was a vital time for them. She couldn't allow anything else to interfere.

Theo seemed to know instinctively how to handle Ari. Suddenly their son was acting more confident and excited about life. Stella had to admit it was wonderful to think Ari had his own real father in his life like his other friends had theirs. She would never have imagined it, but when she saw them together, it was like they'd never been apart.

At one point she would have to let Stasio and Rachel know. The best time to tell them would be when their vacation was over. He already knew something was going on. When he learned the truth, he'd be thrilled for Ari, even with all the bad history.

A boy needed his father. If Theo wanted to fill that role now, Stella had no desire to prevent it. As long as he made Ari happy, then she'd be happy. She was a fool, of course. It was her middle name, otherwise she wouldn't be living for later this afternoon when Theo said he'd be coming to the villa.

After she clicked off, she went back in the cabin.

Theo flicked her a penetrating glance. "Everything all right?"

"Yes. It was Rachel. She was still asleep when we left, so she called to say goodbye."

"We're docking now," Theo murmured. "It's time to walk to the car. Everybody off with their life jackets." Soon they were all put away in the closet.

Ari looked at his father. "Are you going to come with us?"

"I'd like to, but I have a little work to do at the office. The helicopter will fly me into Athens from here and I'll come to the villa later."

"What time?"

"Around four."

Stella walked over to the flowers. "I want to take these with us."

Theo reached for the vase. "I'll empty the water and carry them to the car. Is everybody ready?"

The boys nodded and trooped out first. Stella reached for her purse while Theo brought up the rear. They walked down the passage to the stairs and went below to the next deck. When they reached the car, Theo put the roses in the trunk.

"Looks like you're all set." He came around to Stella's side and squeezed her shoulder. The contact spread fire through every atom of her body. "Drive carefully."

"See you later, Papa."

"See you, Mr. Pantheras."

Stella started the motor and put the car in gear. It was a wrench having to drive away from him. From the sideview mirror she watched him until they'd driven off the ferry.

"Can Dax play at our house when we get home?"

"I've already checked with his mother and it's okay."

"Hooray."

Forty-five minutes later they reached the house. "Aiyee," Iola cried when she saw them enter the kitchen.

Stella was carrying the roses which she took over to the sink. They needed to be put in water again. "We decided to cut our vacation short. Don't worry. Tell the staff I plan to do the cooking and the cleaning around here. You go on doing exactly what you intended to do. We'll try to stay out of your way."

Iola crossed herself. "What's going on?"

Ari gave her a hug. "My papa's coming over this afternoon."

If the housekeeper's eyes grew any bigger, they'd pop. "Your papa?"

"Yup. He's awesome! Come on, Dax. Let's take our stuff upstairs. Do you want me to take up your suitcase, Mom?"

Since when. "Yes. I'd love you to." Wanting to copy his father was a good thing.

"Okay."

Once they disappeared, Stella turned to Iola. "I know what you're thinking. How could I let this happen after that man nearly ruined my life. But this isn't about me."

They walked through the villa to the salon where she set the roses on the coffee table. "Ari has spent quite a bit of time with him and wants to be with him all the time. That's why we're back in Athens so soon."

Iola's hands went to her own cheeks. "I hope you know what you're doing."

"So do I, but you saw Ari just now. There's a new light in his eyes."

"We'll see how long it lasts."

The housekeeper had been through it all with her. Of

course she was fearful. In time she would see what Stella could see right now.

"It's still a secret," she warned her. "No one knows but you and Dax."

"Not Stasio?" She sounded scandalized.

"Not yet. Rachel's nausea has him preoccupied." Though it was true, she knew her brother hadn't been deceived.

Iola shook her head. "He worries over her the way Ari's father should have worried over you!"

"That's in the past, Iola. Ari's happy. I want him to stay that way."

Iola crossed herself again.

# CHAPTER FIVE

IT WAS a novel experience for Theo to be allowed onto Athas property. The guard at the gate let his limo pass through to the front of the square, three-story villa. Built along neoclassic lines, it gave the impression of a temple. In ways it was like a sanctuary, one he'd been forbidden to enter.

But not today. It meant her brothers still didn't know what was going on. He would enjoy his entrée into her world until everything hit the fan. Then he would sit back and watch the spectacle.

At quarter after four he alighted from the limo and bounded up the steps, almost breathless to see Stella. After kissing her on the ferry, he was on fire, and nothing would ever put it out because that was the effect she had on him.

He'd barely rung the doorbell when he heard voices and it opened to reveal his son. They smiled at each other. Dax stood behind him. "Hi, Papa...come on in."

Papa... The most wonderful word he'd ever heard.

"Thanks. Who's your friend?"

The boys laughed.

"Hi."

"Hi, yourself, Dax."

"Mom said to bring you into the salon."

He squeezed Ari's shoulder. "Lead the way."

The elegant interior was what he'd expected of a family of their status, but the only thing that mattered was being with the two people he loved.

"Stella." She looked so gorgeous, the air caught in his lungs. "I like you in yellow." Earlier today she'd been in pink.

A flush swept over her as she looked up from a tray of sodas and snacks she'd just put on the table. The sleeveless top with a matching skirt was sensational on her. "Thank you. Why don't you sit down and we'll talk. Dax, if you'll go to the kitchen, Iola has a snack ready for you. Our meeting won't take long."

"Okay."

Once the three of them were alone, she subsided into a chair facing the couch. Theo guided Ari to it and they sat down together. His son made sure he was supplied something to eat and drink.

"Umm. This baklava is excellent. Thank you. I'm always my hungriest about this time every day."

"Me, too," Ari agreed with him. "We always eat dinner early, huh, Mom."

She nodded. "I thought we ought to talk about plans for the rest of the summer."

"If you don't mind my going first, this might make it easier for you," Theo stated.

"Go ahead."

"As you know," he said, eyeing both of them, "I'm back in Greece with only one agenda, to spend as much time as possible with you."

Ari smiled.

"I want to do what every father wants to do—take you to lessons, the dentist, the doctor, meet your teachers for school this coming fall, plan minivacations, play soccer with you and your friends, shop, go to movies, hang out at my house, just be with you."

"Me, too. Can you stay here and watch *Star Trek* with me tonight?"

"I'd love it. Maybe we could get some takeout for dinner and bring it back while we all watch, but before we plan anything, I want to know what's on your mother's mind. Are you working full-time this summer?"

She put down her soda. "Yes, but I still have two weeks of vacation. Once it's over, I've made an arrangement with Keiko. He'll work from nine to five. I'll plan to go in at six-thirty every day so I can be home by two-thirty. I've planned for Ari to do some reading and math at the next session of summer school in the mornings."

"But I don't want to go to school."

"It's a good idea, Ari," Theo backed her up. "You need to keep your mind active. I was thinking we could get ourselves enrolled in a young astronomers program, too."

"What's that?" He jumped off the couch too excited to sit still.

"I'm sure some of the colleges have them. You look through a telescope and they teach you about the stars."

"Could I do that, Mom?"

"Of course."

"If you would bring me your telephone book, we could call around and see what's being offered."

"I'll get it."

After he dashed out of the room Theo sat forward. "Stella? Look at me for a minute." She lifted her head. "I hope you know I'm not trying to usurp your place. I want to help ease the burden of all you have to do. Look on me as your support system, a permanent one. I'll do whatever you'd like. If I'm overwhelming you, tell me."

She got to her feet. "You're not. It's what Ari wants. I can't deny that Ari is a changed boy already. That's all because of you."

"Thank you for saying that."

She held on to the back of the chair. "All his life he's been surrounded by other children who live with a father and mother. However, I didn't think he noticed that much or cared, not with Stasio, who has been wonderful to him."

Only because he and Nikos had stolen Ari from him. The bile rose in Theo's throat.

"You have no conception of how changed he is. Otherwise he would never have begged to leave Andros where he could have Stasio's constant attention. He didn't even say goodbye to his uncle, the man he has always depended on."

Theo liked hearing it, but when Stasio found out what was going on, there was going to be a showdown. This time Theo was ready for whatever the Athas family had to throw at him.

"His need to be with you supercedes all else," Stella confessed. "There's a new confidence about him. That's because he knows his real father loves him. I have to admit I can't be sorry about that. In truth I've always had to help Ari work on his confidence."

Puzzled, Theo got to his feet. "What are you talking about?"

She rubbed her hands together, a sure sign of nervousness. "It's a long story. You need to hear everything so you'll understand Ari's psyche. I'll tell you after he goes to bed tonight."

He had a feeling that whatever she had to say to him was going to turn his guts inside out all over again. Though he wanted to press her, he could hear the boys coming.

"Here's the directory, Papa." Dax came in with him.

"Terrific. Let me make a few calls and we'll see what's available."

Ari eyed him expectantly while he made inquiries. Eventually he hung up and said, "We're in luck. There's a star-gazing program that started this week, but we can join in on Friday evening, so I have an idea.

"Why don't we visit the college in the morning. After we've registered for the session, we'll fly to St. Thomas for the day."

"Hey," Dax piped up. "My parents went there a couple of weeks ago. My dad loves golf. He said the resort has the best golf course he ever played on."

That was nice to hear. "Have either of you ever played?"

Both boys shook their heads.

"How about you, Stella?"

"No."

"Then we'll make up a foursome and do nine holes. How does that sound?"

"Cool." Ari high-fived his friend.

Stella's mouth lifted at the corners. "Ari? Why don't you show your father to the family room upstairs to watch your DVD."

"Okay. Come on, Papa."

His gaze held hers. "Before we do anything, I'll go pick up some food for us. You guys can come if you want to help me choose."

"That's not necessary, Theo. We have plenty of food here. Ari and Dax can carry it up when you get hungry."

"Then bring on the starship *Enterprise,*" he said before tearing his eyes from hers.

The five-hour marathon with the boys entertained him no end. Stella slipped in and out with sandwiches and salad, but he was glad when she finally insisted the boys go to bed. Until she explained what she'd meant earlier, he would have no peace.

As soon as she joined him in the salon, he said, "What's this about Ari not having confidence?"

Once again she sat down opposite him. "Let me give you some background. After what happened at the church, my grief made me ill. There was too much tension in the house. My father was upset that I'd gotten involved with you, and Nikos's attitude made everything so much worse. Stasio had to leave for New York on business and took me with him.

"I lived in his apartment both before and after I had the baby. He hired a Greek couple to help me when he couldn't be home. He also made it possible for me to attend college and get my business degree there."

Nothing she'd just told him added up to what he'd been thinking about Stasio. Had Theo been wrong about him?

"You're an amazing woman." He was proud of what she'd accomplished, but he could hardly hold on to his rage over events he'd been helpless to prevent at the time.

She shook her head. "No. Thousands of women do the same thing every day. Once I'd graduated, I told Stasio I wanted to go back to Greece and get a job. Ari was old enough to attend kindergarten and I could work out my schedule with Iola's help.

"Everything went well except that in returning to Athens, it brought us back into Nikos's orbit. He never accepted Ari and it showed. The last couple of years have been hard on our son.

"Though Ari doesn't understand why, he's aware of the way Nikos feels and goes to great lengths not to antagonize him for fear of being mocked or ridiculed. As a result, he doesn't always show a lot of confidence. That's what I wanted you to understand." Tears prickled against her eyelids. "For him to finally have his own father who champions him is making all the difference."

He got to his feet. "None of this should have happened," he muttered. More and more he was beginning to think the cruelty was all on Nikos's part. "Though there's nothing we can do about the past, I swear to you I'll never let any harm or hurt come to you or Ari again."

"Theo," she cried in abject frustration. "If you want me to believe you, you have to confide in me completely about the past. No lies."

"If you'll do me one favor first, then I promise to tell you details."

When she closed her eyes, tears squeezed out. "What favor?" she whispered.

"Tell your brothers I've returned to Greece and have been seeing you and Ari." There was going to be an explosion, one Stella needed to experience to understand.

A stillness surrounded her before she got up from the chair. "I don't want them to know yet because this is a very precarious time for you and Ari. I've been waiting to see how things would go. Naturally, I plan to tell them."

"But you're afraid to tell them. I can see it in your eyes. I don't blame you. We always had to hide our love from your family, but we were young then. Now we're two mature adults with a six-year-old son. There's nothing to be afraid of. I'm here to protect you. Does

Ari know how you and I used to have to sneak around to be together?"

"No. As I told you before, he knows nothing about my turmoil."

"I'm indebted to you for that. It's the reason he and I have been able to bond so fast. For that very reason he'll think it's strange if you're not straightforward with your family."

"You're right. It's just that—"

"What?" he broke in. "Are you afraid they're going to object?"

She bit her lower lip, the one he wanted to kiss. "You hurt me. I was their younger sister."

"But we were torn from each other in the most cruel way possible. Surely that would make a difference to any sane, rational person." What she couldn't know was that he didn't put Nikos in that category.

"I'm not ready to say anything quite yet. In a couple of weeks Stasio will be back from vacation. Then I'll tell him." She shook her head, causing her dark hair to swish. "I have to tell him at the right time."

Theo realized she was terrified because he would always be a Pantheras in their eyes and she knew her family would never approve. She had every reason to want to put it off.

"Tell them soon, Stella," he urged, afraid it fell on deaf ears. "We don't want Ari hurt by this if he doesn't have to be. I'm leaving now. My limo's waiting. I'll be by for you at ten tomorrow."

He strode out of the house without looking back. She was too much of a temptation for him to be alone with her in the same room any longer.

\* \* \*

The next morning Stella ate breakfast with the boys, aware of an excitement building inside her she couldn't control. After going back and forth, she chose to wear white cargo pants and a sleeveless lime-green top that tied at the shoulders. There was no use pretending she didn't care what Theo thought. She had her pride and wanted to look beautiful for him.

While she was putting on lipstick, her phone rang. Theo? Her heart thudded as she reached for her cell. It turned out to be Dax's mom. She'd be by at dinnertime to pick him up.

They chatted for a minute before Stella hung up to brush her hair. She had an idea Dax wasn't ready to go home yet. He'd been enjoying Theo's company too much. Ari on the other hand would be thrilled to finally get his daddy to himself.

Twenty minutes later he appeared at the villa. Stella stepped outside and got in the limo next to him. She could feel him studying her. While the boys chattered, she and Theo made desultory conversation. After visiting the campus, they headed for Theo's office.

Once they rode the elevator to the roof, they got in the helicopter. Boris was already onboard and everyone got acquainted. Soon they were airborne. She smiled at Ari. "Are you excited about your stargazing class?"

"Yup. It's going to be awesome."

*Awesome* was a word that covered everything fun or wonderful. The class started at nine o'clock and went three times a week for two more weeks.

"I'm sure it will be fascinating."

Theo sat in the copilot's seat looking at home there with

headgear on. "As soon as we land, are you guys ready for golf or do you want to play on the water slide first?"

"I didn't know it had one of those." Dax sounded euphoric.

"It's guaranteed to curl your hair."

Everyone laughed. Even Stella. She could trust Theo, couldn't she? Ari did, wholeheartedly. For the rest of the day she was determined to put all doubts behind her and just enjoy the moment.

As soon as she made that decision, her body started to relax, enabling her to entertain feelings she'd been forced to suppress since she'd first seen him at the paddleboat concession.

He had the kind of hard-muscled body that looked good in anything. Today he'd worn a magenta sport shirt and cream-colored trousers that rode low on his hips. Theo was unaware of his masculine charisma. She, on the other hand, had trouble keeping her eyes off him.

Years ago every girl at church had woven a fantasy about him. Stella hadn't been able to believe it when he'd sit behind her in Sunday school and whisper things to her while the priest gave a lesson. When they went into mass, he'd sit in the same row and lean forward so he could smile at her.

Whatever activity, he came and made certain they were together in some capacity. Her friends thought he was sexy and told her how lucky she was. Stella knew it, but with her family looking on, she had to be careful they didn't find out what was happening.

When the church had put on a festival to raise money, he had chosen her as his partner to perform a folk dance. There were practices and they had to wear costumes. The thrill of those moments while they got ready for the big night still set her pulse racing. He'd dance too close and kiss her hair. Theo drove her crazy with all his attention. She loved him with a passion that broke down her inhibitions.

Their son, Ari, sitting next to her was proof that she'd loved Theo body and soul. She hadn't been able to hold back her desire. That period had been filled with the greatest ecstasy imaginable. Then it had ended so abruptly in one night, something in her had died.

She realized she'd been dead for years. Now suddenly he was back. Despite the things she didn't know, something inside her had leaped to life again, portending something bigger and brighter than before. Yesterday in the cabin on the ferry, she'd forgotten everything in the sheer joy of being in his arms again.

"Stella?" The voice infiltrating her body jerked her from her intimate thoughts.

"What is it?"

"We've landed." So they had. "The boys have run ahead to set up our golf game." She noticed that the pilot and Boris had already exited, too. "Do you need help?"

He looked as if he was going to come back and start removing the straps one kiss at a time. Her cheeks grew warm at the direction of her thoughts. If someone saw them… "No, thank you. I can manage."

After unstrapping herself, she moved to the entrance where he swung her to the ground. He did it slowly, causing her body to slide down his, creating delicious heat between them. Yesterday they'd had the life jackets between them, but no longer. She quickly hurried ahead of him, but her legs felt like mush.

As they got closer, she saw the boys come out the doors of the clubhouse with two bags of clubs, but they weren't alone. A shudder rocked her body. To her shock it was Nikos with his longtime Swiss ski buddy Fritz walking behind them. Her secret was out now to the one person she hadn't wanted to know anything!

Who would have thought she'd bump into her brother here? Except that it wasn't a complete surprise. Nikos loved golf when he wasn't skiing. He said the mental game kept him sharp. Was Renate with him, or had he left her on Andros for the day?

She watched him take Ari aside and engage him in conversation. Even as far apart as they still were, she could tell her son was being vetted. Dax stood by Fritz. She'd have given anything if things hadn't happened this way, but there was no help for it now.

Fritz came forward and gave her a kiss on both cheeks. "Stella Athas. It's been a few years. Nikos didn't tell me you'd grown into such a raving beauty."

She'd never cared for his brash manner and didn't like the way he was checking her out. "How are you, Fritz? Let me introduce you to Ari's father, Theo Pantheras. Theo? Fritz here took the bronze for Switzerland in the slalom a few years ago."

"Hello." Theo shook his hand without saying anything else. Most people fawned over Fritz and Nikos, but she knew Theo wasn't as easily impressed.

Ari walked over to stand next to Theo who put his arms around him and hugged him close in a protective gesture. It thrilled Stella. Her son now had his own dad, thank heaven. Nikos couldn't say or do anything about it.

Her brother trained his eyes on her and came closer. They glittered in that icy way they did when his anger was truly kindled. "Well, well, well. A day of golf for my little sister."

Nikos didn't even pretend to acknowledge Theo. Six years had done nothing to teach her brother a thing about human decency. His behavior now reminded her of one time in New York when he'd humiliated Rachel so thoroughly, Stella had thought she'd lost her best friend for good. He'd called her a fat, orange-haired, American military brat in her hearing. Stella had never forgiven him for hurting her friend.

"Who would have imagined finding you on the world's newest and most celebrated golf course?"

"I was about to say the same thing," she said, daring to speak her mind again. It was cathartic to be able to. "Where's Renate?"

"With Rachel," he muttered. "Since you left Andros so fast, I think it's time you and I had a little talk to catch up. If the rest of you will excuse us for a few minutes."

"Maybe another time," Theo interjected smoothly. "We don't want to be late for our tee-off time."

Nothing would have enraged Nikos more than to be snubbed in front of Fritz like that, by Theo no less. She could feel her brother seething. Theo on the other hand seemed to care less.

He put his other arm around Stella's shoulders. "Come on, everyone—Dax—" he urged the boy hauling the other golf bag. Together the four of them headed for the first tee.

"Stella? I'm waiting." Nikos said coldly.

In order to prevent a contretemps, she decided to talk to him, but Theo stopped her from moving. "I'm afraid you'll be waiting a long time. It appears the two of you will have to have one of your family chats another time. She and the boys are with me and we're busy."

Her brother came closer. "I could have you thrown

off this resort for talking to me that way," he snarled at Theo. "One word to the owner from me and that's that."

"Stop it, Nikos," Stella muttered, mortified and infuriated by his behavior. He was out of control. Even with the boys around, he didn't care what they thought of him.

"I will, after we've had our talk." He wouldn't let this go. It was unbelievable.

She felt Theo remove his arm and pull out his cell phone. Whatever he said was short and to the point. Almost immediately she saw Theo's bodyguard and another man coming toward them from the clubhouse at full speed.

"Boris? If you would see that these two gentlemen leave the course, we'd be grateful."

Nikos was a skier, not a body builder. The two men could take care of him with no problem. Part of her was thrilled to see him thwarted, but another part grieved for him. He was her brother and she loved him, but it had been years since she'd liked him. She had to search back in her memory when he was a preteen to remember anything good.

"Who in the hell do you think you are?" Nikos demanded.

"Nikos," Stella cried, "what's the matter with you?"

"It's all right," Theo assured her. "He's just surprised to see me with you again after all these years, aren't you, Nikos. Better get used to it since the blood of our two families runs through Ari's veins.

"If you can learn to behave yourself, you're welcome to golf here again another time when you've cooled down. My treat. I'm the owner. Now we really have to get cracking, don't we Ari."

Her son smiled. "Yes. See ya, Uncle Nikos." When

they'd walked a little distance, Ari looked up at him. "I didn't know you owned this place."

"There's a lot you don't know about me, or me you. That's why it's so great we're planning to spend as much time together as possible, don't you think?"

"Yes." He was beaming. "Mom? I've never seen Uncle Nikos so mad."

She was still shivering. It was truth time. "Unfortunately I've seen him worse, honey. We'll just stay away from him for a while until he apologizes."

"He doesn't like me."

That was the first time Ari had admitted it aloud. All because of his father, who'd given him new confidence.

"It's *me* he doesn't like, Ari," Theo said softly.

"How come?"

"I come from a very poor family. Your uncle didn't like me being with your mother or having anything to do with her."

"That's stupid."

"I agree, but a lot of wealthy people like your uncle feel that way."

"Uncle Nikos isn't wealthy. Uncle Stasi has to give him money when he runs out."

A gasp escaped Stella's lips. Ari knew too much for his own good.

"Well, let's forget it and have ourselves a fun game. Who wants to go first?"

"I do," Stella volunteered. After the awful scene with Nikos, she needed to do something physical to channel all that negative energy in a different direction.

"This is going to be an adventure," Theo whispered against her neck. All her anxiety flew out the window as other sensations took over.

He'd already put his arms around her to demonstrate how to do a golf swing. The weight of his hard body cocooning hers caused her to forget what she was doing. She felt him nibble her sun-warmed shoulder where the tie had slipped a little. It made her breathless.

"How soon is it going to be our turn?" Ari stood next to Dax, resigned it might be a long wait.

He'd asked it so seriously, she and Theo burst out laughing at the same time. It suddenly occurred to her she hadn't been this happy in years. He'd brought joy to his son's life. He'd slain a dragon for her today. A week ago she couldn't have imagined any of it.

Please, God. Don't let the darkness come again. Make this happiness last.

# CHAPTER SIX

AT SIX that evening, Stella walked Dax out to his parents' car. Ari and Theo followed with his suitcase and the games and stuff he'd brought with him. Everyone hugged. Dax gave Theo a super-duper hug.

In front of Dax's parents, Theo invited Ari's friend to come to Salamis Island in a couple of weekends for a sleepover. The other man nodded his agreement of the idea. They chatted about the golf course for a few minutes.

"I love you guys," Dax said to Stella before giving her a hug. "I had an awesome time."

"It was a treat for us, too, honey," she told him. With Theo around it couldn't have been anything else.

Elani stared at Theo before flashing Stella a private message. She could hear her friend asking where *he'd* come from. Not even Elani was immune. Dax would fill her in on some of the details. The rest would have to wait until Stella phoned her friend and confided in her.

When the three of them went back into the house, Ari turned to her. "Now that Dax has gone home, can papa sleep in my room tonight? Please?"

Stella should have seen it coming, but the thought of Theo staying over made her heart skip a couple of beats.

"What do you say, Stella?" Theo teased gently.

He probably sensed how much she wanted him to stay. Maybe it would be a good thing. Maybe they could really talk after Ari went to bed. She was finally in a mood to listen. "It's all right with me, but only if you don't tell UFO stories and keep each other awake all night."

Ari launched himself at her. "Thanks, Mom." His eyes looked suspiciously bright in the foyer light. "I love you."

"I love you, too, honey."

"This was the best day of my life!"

He said that every time he'd been with Theo. She believed it.

His father grabbed him. "And it's not over yet!"

"Come on upstairs, Papa."

Stella nodded to him. "I'll be up in a minute to bring you a few things." While she was at it she'd find one of Stasio's robes for Theo to wear. He was a tall, powerfully built man like Theo. They'd be hanging in Stasio's closet.

"Hurry," he whispered with urgency in his voice before racing Ari up the stairs two at a time. They whooped it up like two kids. Their laughter floated down and followed her to the kitchen.

Iola came rushing in. "What's going on? I thought Dax went home."

She gathered some fruit and chips for them. "He did, but now we have another guest."

"Who?"

"Ari's father."

She crossed herself. "Aiyee—"

Stella chuckled. "It's all right. I'm glad they're together. A boy should be with his father."

"That isn't what you thought last week."

"A lot has changed since then. He's come back to stay, Iola."

"You have forgiven him?"

She sucked in her breath. "Yes." *Until I know differently.*

"What if he disappears again?"

"He won't." She knew that in her heart even if she didn't know all of it. Theo had convinced her that Ari meant everything to him. She had to believe him. She would go on believing it.

"How long is he going to stay here?"

"I don't really know yet. He and Ari have a lot of stuff to catch up on."

"And you, too?"

"Maybe."

"Just don't get hurt again."

If it was going to happen, the advice had come too late. "Don't fuss about anything, Iola. We'll just be lazing around here for a few days." Ari needed a taste of what it was like to be around his father all the time.

"But what if your brothers come home for some reason?"

"It doesn't matter." Now that Nikos had seen them together, it wouldn't be long before he told Stasio. In a way it was just as well. With the word out, both brothers would have time to get used to the idea. Once she told Stasio how happy Ari was, he'd be his loving, understanding self.

She had this dream that one day Theo and Stasio would become good friends in their own right, and not just because of Ari, whom they both adored. Though the two men were almost ten years apart, they had the strongest work ethic she'd ever seen. Best of all, they were both intrinsically kind and loved Ari.

"Good night, Iola."

Stella darted off to her room. She was pretty sure there was an extra toothbrush in the bathroom cupboard. She also had some throwaway razors Theo could have if he wanted.

Once she'd found everything and made a detour to Stasio's room, she hurried to Ari's room.

"Hi, Mom. I'm showing papa my scrapbooks so he can see what I looked like when I was a baby." They sat on the bed side by side, poring over everything.

She laid things down on the end of the other queen-size bed. "Those are precious photos."

"Amen." Theo's voice grated with deep emotion. She knew why. He hadn't been there for any of it. He patted the side of the bed next to him so she'd join them. "Ari's been telling me about the couple who lived with you in New York. I want to meet them."

"They're marvelous people."

"They were really nice, Papa."

"And lucky," Theo added. "They got to hold you all the time, change your diapers, tell you stories and kiss you when you cried. I'm jealous."

It wrenched Stella's heart that Theo had missed out on all of it. She felt his hand slide around her waist and squeeze her hip. "I'll be eternally grateful to them for helping your mom when I couldn't. One day we'll fly to New York so I can meet them."

"Could we?" Ari cried.

"We'll do a lot of things."

Stella was curious to know what kinds of things he had in mind, but she would have to ask him later. "I think it's time you got ready for bed," she reminded Ari.

"Okay."

"Theo, I brought you a robe and a couple of other items. You can use Ari's bathroom to change."

"Thank you." His eyes captured hers. "This is what I call living!" He got up from the bed and disappeared into the bathroom.

Ari slipped on his pajamas in record time. "Mom? Can Papa stay with us all the time?"

"I'm afraid not, honey."

"How come?"

Floundering, she said, "Because he has his own house. Like you, I'm getting used to having him in my life again."

His eyes shone. "But you like him."

"You know I do."

"I love him."

"I kind of figured that out."

"I'm so glad he came back."

"I'm glad, too," she admitted. Her son was a different person. "Good night, honey."

She kissed his forehead, then rushed to her own room to get ready for bed. Stella couldn't imagine how she would get to sleep knowing Theo was next door. The knowledge that they'd be spending tomorrow together made her even more excited.

After slipping on a nightgown, she went into the bathroom to brush her teeth. Once she'd turned off the light, she had every intention of going to bed. However, she heard their voices carry because she shared a bathroom with Ari. Though she hated herself for eavesdropping, she couldn't resist listening at the door for a second.

"...because I felt inferior to my brother. Hektor was the oldest in my family and had a calling for the priesthood. My parents loved him so much, I thought they didn't love me."

"Did it make you cry?"

"A lot when I was really young."

"I love you, Papa."

"I know you do. I love you, too. More than anything on earth."

"Did your other brothers feel bad, too?"

"I think so, but I never talked to them about it. When he left our house for good, it was very hard on me. I'd lost my big brother. About that time I made plans to go away with your mother and marry her, but the night we were going to meet at the church, some mean guys beat me up."

"How come, Papa?" he cried in a tear-filled voice. "Why did they do that?"

"Because they didn't like me and wanted to keep me and your mother apart. They got their wish."

Stella felt bile rise in her throat. Who was responsible for such a crime? Who would have cared to that degree?

"When I got better, I looked everywhere for your mother. My friends and family helped me. I made phone calls and sent her letters, but no one had seen her and I realized I'd really lost her."

"She went to New York with Stasi."

"I know that now, but at the time it was like she'd never existed. Suffice it to say that when I lost her, I lost my very best friend."

Tears gushed down her cheeks. *You were mine, too, Theo.*

"And because I lost her, I lost you."

"I'm here now, Papa."

"Don't I know it. Unfortunately back then, I was in a very bad way. That's when I decided to leave home and start working on a career, but it was the most painful time in my life. I never thought I'd see her again, but then I drove by your house last week and saw both of you walking. I couldn't believe it! It made me so happy, I wrote your mother a letter and asked her to call me."

"But Mommy thought you didn't love her anymore."

"I realize that now, but it wasn't true. I loved your mommy so much I would have done anything for her. But I had to make money so I could pay someone to help me find her."

"Because you were poor, huh."

"Yes, because I'm a Pantheras from the poor part of Salamis and Stella was an Athas from the best part of Athens."

"I'm a Pantheras, too!" Ari declared.

"Yes you are, half me, half your mom, and none of it matters as long as we're all together."

She couldn't take any more and went back to her room. Theo had told her there were things she still didn't know that could hurt her and Ari. Had her father been so against her marrying Theo, *he* was the one behind the attack?

Stella's father had been a very stern man who'd risen to prominence in the Greek government. He was very proper, old-fashioned. His pride had always made it difficult for her to approach him about her personal life.

When she thought about it, he had many influential friends in high places. Had he arranged things behind the scenes, never expecting Theo to come back and fight for his son? Deep down, had he been a corrupt man?

If so, and Nikos knew about it, then it would explain why her brother had been so obnoxious at the golf course. It was almost as if he were carrying on where her father had left off, but he was blatantly open about it. Stasio would have been kept in the dark. She knew for a fact he would never have sanctioned anything cruel or criminal. It wasn't in his nature.

Was that why Theo was afraid to tell her, because he didn't want her to hate her father?

For the rest of the night her mind ran in circles, driving her crazy with more questions until she knew no more. By morning she was worn out. When Ari came to her room and begged her to let his daddy stay at their house through the weekend, she couldn't say no. They were all on vacation and her brothers were on Andros.

Every day Ari spent with his father in their house, she could see that he was becoming more secure. Between walks around Athens and their star-gazing class, there was plenty to do that was all new to him. Theo had opened up a different world for him, and her son was having the time of his life.

Before bed on Saturday night, Stella sought out Iola. "Tell cook we'll be wanting a big breakfast in the morning before we go to church."

Stella dashed upstairs and discovered Ari and his father watching a DVD about the day the earth stood still. A smile broke out on her face. "Hi, guys. Considering our plans for tomorrow, you'd better get to bed soon. In the meantime, I need to check and make sure your suit is ready for church, Ari."

She went to his room and walked inside his closet. The pants of his navy three-piece could use a pressing. She pulled them out. The jacket looked fine. After an inspection she discovered both dress shirts had been washed and ironed.

"I like the blue-and-white stripe the best," Theo murmured right behind her. A little cry of surprise broke from her throat. Except for the day he'd helped her with her golf swing, he hadn't made any kind of overture toward her. When he slid his arms around her, bringing her back up tight against his chest, it took her totally by surprise. He'd already changed into his robe.

For quite a while now she'd been so aware of him physically, it had become painful to be near him. With a sense of wonder she felt him kiss her nape, sending little fingers of delight inching their way through her body. She grew weak with those old, breathtaking feelings of desire.

"What a wonderful place to find you," he whispered in a husky voice. In the next instant he'd turned her around so their faces were mere centimeters apart. "I don't know about you, but if I can't have this right now, I'm not going to survive the night."

His dark head descended, covering her mouth with his own. Surrounded by clothes that muffled sounds, he kissed her with a hunger that brought a moan to her throat.

Back and forth they returned each other's kisses, setting off waves of desire. He smelled wonderfully male, intoxicating her. As her hands slid up his chest, she came in contact with a smattering of black hair.

The feel of his skin electrified her, bringing back memories she couldn't afford to entertain with Ari just outside the door. This was crazy. Insane. She wrenched her lips from his. "We can't do this."

His deep chuckle thrilled her. "It appears we are." He kissed her again, long and deep until she was a throbbing mass of needs. He undid one of the ties to kiss her shoulder. Rapture exploded inside her, but she knew where this was leading and finally backed out of the closet, gasping for air.

"Did you forget these?" He dangled Ari's pants in

front of her while she retied her blouse on top of her shoulder. His wolfish grin was the last straw. She took the pants and threw them at him. Ari roared with laughter.

Theo ducked, then swiped them from the floor. "You better watch out, little girl. You're playing with a big boy now."

She screamed and ran away from him. Ari was jumping on top of the bed with a huge smile while he watched them. Stella backed up against the wall. Theo came closer, twirling the pants in the air. He looked dark and dangerous and capable of doing anything.

"Wh-what are you going to do?" She stumbled over the words.

His eyes narrowed. "What you'd like me to do."

"Get her and tickle her, Papa. She hates to be tickled."

"Traitor!"

"Thanks for the tip, son." Except that Theo already knew about her ticklish side.

"No, Theo… Please."

He came at her anyway with a frightening growl. While she tried to dodge him, Iola came to the door with an anxious look. "Is everything all right?"

"No." Stella grinned. "I'm getting tickled to death."

The housekeeper's frown actually turned into a smile. Stella couldn't remember the last time she'd seen one of those from her.

"Good night, but keep the noise down so people around here can sleep!"

"Sorry, Iola," Theo called out. Ari echoed him.

Stella turned to the men. "I'll say good night, too."

"Don't go yet," Theo whispered, but she didn't dare linger. Quick as lightning she grabbed the pants before closing the door. Tomorrow she'd press them.

After giving Iola a hug, she went to her room but couldn't imagine how she would get to sleep after being thoroughly kissed in Theo's arms. The knowledge that they'd be spending tomorrow together caused her body to ache with longing. And trepidation, too.

They were going to church tomorrow to meet Theo's family, and the only reason she was going to be introduced to them after all these years was because of Ari. His parents had never approved of his association with Stella. Knowing that, Theo had never taken her home to meet them. It was all very sad.

She could only hope they would learn to tolerate her for Ari's sake. No matter what Theo might have told them, Stella was the reason Theo had left Greece in the first place. That wouldn't exactly have endeared her to them, but Ari would win them over.

When Theo had returned to Greece, he'd received a blessing from his oldest brother, who was one of the priests at the church in the Plaka near the cathedral. To Theos mind, Hektor had never looked more impressive than in his vestments.

Their reunion had been a heartwarming one. They had spent part of the day together catching up on each other's lives. There was laughter and weeping followed by a serious talk about Stella and Ari. Theo promised his brother that when and if he could, he would bring them both to the church to meet him.

That day had come.

Following the mass, his brother had invited Theo's family into his private study in the old house next to the church. He shared it with two other priests who had apartments there.

"Come in here."

Theo was the last to enter the room with Stella and Ari. He was proud to be able to introduce them. Like his son, he'd dressed in a navy suit that went with the sobriety of the occasion. Stella looked a vision in a summery two-piece hyacinth suit, elegantly tailored. Her coloring added to the picture of classy femininity.

He ushered them over to the couch where the family had congregated. Theo's parents couldn't take their eyes off Stella and Ari. His brothers and their families were equally dazzled.

"As you can all see, I brought a surprise today," Theo began. "Stella? Ari? I'd like you to meet my family starting with my mother, Ariadne, and my father, Gregory."

His mother beamed at both of them. "I've wanted to meet you for a long time."

"I have, too," Stella responded quietly.

Her gaze rested on her grandson. "You and I have the same name."

"I know." Ari smiled as he moved around the room with Stella to shake everyone's hand.

Theo's father studied him. "You look so much like my Theo, I think I'm seeing things."

"We have the same peak," Ari said, pointing to his hair. Everyone laughed.

"This is my brother Dymas, his wife Lina and their children, Calli, Dori and Spiro."

Ari eyed his older cousins. "Hi."

"Hi," they all said in turn.

"This is my brother Spiro, his wife, Minta, and their children Phyllis, Roxane and Leandros."

Ari looked at Theo before he said, "He's the one my age, huh."

"Right. You're both six going on a hundred."

Everyone laughed again.

"Last but not least, my oldest brother Hektor, Father Matthias."

Ari walked up to him and shook his hand. "Papa said he misses you a lot."

Hektor seemed moved. "I'm not supposed to admit it, but I miss all of my family, too."

"Do you like being a priest?"

He smiled. "Very much. I'm so happy you and your father have been united. He didn't know he had a son. What a wonderful present to come home to. He loves you very much."

"I love him, too!"

"If you don't mind, I'd like to give you a blessing. Is that all right with you?"

Ari nodded.

It was a short blessing, sweet and it brought a lump to Theo's throat. He eyed Stella out of the corner of his eye. Her head was bowed. He could tell the words had touched her, too.

After a few more minutes they all said goodbye and climbed into two limos Theo had provided for the family. He and Stella rode with his parents and Ari. They headed to Salamis. During the drive everyone got a little better acquainted. His father laughed more than he'd heard him in a long time.

By the time they ate dinner at the *taverna,* spirits were high. Theo could tell Stella and Ari were enjoying themselves. His son went off with Leandros for a little while, breaking the ice even more.

Stella chatted with his sisters-in-law about their children. The subject was something they could all relate to. As far as he could tell, there were no uncom-fortable moments.

"It was a good beginning, don't you think?" Theo asked Stella during their trip back to Athens via the linking road from Perama to the mainland. She was seated across from him next to Ari.

"We had a wonderful time." With Ari along, she couldn't ask Theo how his parents really felt.

"Yeah, but I wish I didn't have to wear this suit all day long."

Theo threw his head back and laughed. "You're so much like me it hurts. I promise you won't have to wear one until we go to church again."

He eyed Theo soberly. "Do you like church?"

Stella glanced at him, waiting to hear his answer.

"Honestly?"

Ari nodded.

"I don't exactly like it, but I always feel better after I've gone."

"Is that how you feel, too, Mom?"

Now the shoe was on the other foot. He grinned while she decided what to say.

"Yes."

"But how did you feel when you were my age?"

She chuckled. "I didn't like it all that much."

"You see why I loved your mother so much, Ari? We think alike."

"I bet you wouldn't tell Hektor that."

"He knew how I felt when I was little because I squirmed all the time. I didn't have to say anything."

"He was nice. So are my grandparents."

"I'm glad you feel that way because they're crazy about you."

"They want me to come and see them next week. Grandma said I could help them in the kitchen."

"Would you like that?"

"I'd love it!"

"Then we'll definitely go over. While your mom and I have dinner, you can serve us before we have to leave for our class."

"That would be awesome. Leandros wishes he could come with us."

"Maybe sometime we can arrange it. We'll have to check with the staff at the college. Does he like UFO stuff?"

"Yeah. He's pretty cool."

High praise. Theo's cup was running over tonight.

"Can you sleep at our house again tonight, Papa?" They'd just driven up in front of the villa.

Without looking at Stella he said, "I have a much better idea. Since your mother still has ten days of vacation left, why don't the three of us take our own vacation on St. Thomas? I haven't been on a real one in years. I can promise you we'll never run out of things to do."

Ari looked like he was going to burst with joy. "Could we, Mom?"

Theo could tell he'd surprised Stella with his suggestion, but knowing she would have to think about it, he would give her the time because it had been a perfect day and he refused to ruin it.

"Tell you what, Ari. I have some business to do and will probably work at my office until I pick you up for our class tomorrow. Afterward, we'll fly to St. Thomas, that is if your mother approves."

"Can we, Mom? Please?"

"I…I think that sounds exciting," her voice faltered.

Until she'd said the words, Theo hadn't realized he'd been holding his breath. "While you guys pack, I'll get my work out of the way so I can concentrate on you for the next ten days."

"I can't wait, but I wish I could come to your office and see what you do."

"Another time and you can. We've got the rest of our lives, Ari."

"Your father's right," Stella interjected. "He's a busy man and you have to respect that."

"What are you going to do tomorrow, Mom?"

"Lots of errands to get ready for our trip."

"I'd rather go with you in our new car."

As she laughed, her eyes happened to meet Theo's. For the first time he felt they were communicating like they once did, sharing the same joy. It was a moment he wanted to freeze.

If he weren't afraid of losing the ground he'd gained, he would take her and Ari to St. Thomas in the morning, but he didn't want to push Stella. Though his work could wait, he pretended otherwise and kept silent, endeavoring to avoid Ari's pleading look. Nothing would please him more than to keep Ari at his office with him, but again, Stella needed time to get used to Theo being in her life again.

Once he'd undone his seat belt, he got out to help them to the front door. "Good night, son." He gave Ari a bear hug.

"Sleep well, Stella." He darted her a penetrating glance before getting back in the limo. After the day they'd spent together, he didn't dare touch her.

## CHAPTER SEVEN

WHILE Stella got ready for bed, her mind was on Theo. Today had been a great highlight for her meeting his family, going to church with them. But when he'd brought her and Ari home, she'd sensed a certain reticence on his part to linger. It was impossible to know what was going on inside him. She was afraid, but didn't know of what exactly.

Yes she did. Deep down she knew he didn't want to tell her about her father. Theo was afraid that when he shared that with her, it would devastate her. Maybe it would when confronted with the irrefutable proof, but her austere father had passed on. What was important was Ari's relationship with Theo. No one could hurt that now.

Before she slipped under the covers, she reached for her phone to check any messages. Afraid it would ring while they were in church, she'd turned it off and had forgotten about it. When she looked now, she noticed three from Rachel. Each one begged her to call immediately, no matter how late.

Fearing this had to do with her pregnancy, Stella phoned. Rachel answered right away. "Thank you for calling!" she cried anxiously.

She clutched the phone tighter. "Is there something wrong with the baby?"

"No. Stella—why didn't you tell us about Theo while you were here? When Nikos flew back from St. Thomas the other night, it was all he could talk about."

A band constricted her lungs. "It's exactly for that reason I didn't want anyone to know anything."

"Know what?"

Rachel was Stella's oldest, closest friend. She trusted her with her life. Without preamble she told her everything. When she'd finished, the silence on the other end was deafening.

"Rachel? Are you still there?"

"Yes. Oh, Stella—"

"I know what you're thinking, but…I trust him. He was beaten up. You can see the damage. I think my father had something to do with it."

"You're kidding—"

"No. I've had time to think it all out. At the right moment, I'll get the truth from Theo. In the meantime, don't tell Stasio my suspicions. He revered father so much, it could really hurt him." In fact, the truth would hurt him a lot more than it was hurting Stella right now.

"You honestly believe Theo, don't you."

"Yes, Rachel. You'd have to see him with Ari to understand."

"Well if it's good enough for you, then it is for me, too."

Tears welled up. "Thank you, dear friend. You couldn't possibly know what that means to me."

"Your happiness is everything. Stasio feels the same way. Unfortunately, Nikos keeps talking about your parents and how upset they would be if they knew you'd been seeing him again. He blames your father's heart attack on your association with Theo. Maybe Nikos was in your father's confidence."

"I'm thinking the same thing," she whispered. "The point is, it happened a long time ago. With father gone, this is no longer any of Nikos's business. Not that it ever was, but if father told Nikos how he felt about Theo, then it makes a sick kind of sense."

"I agree. Is it true Theo owns that new resort on St. Thomas?"

"Yes."

"You might as well hear the rest, then. Nikos told Stasio he believes Theo is tied to underworld crime, otherwise he couldn't possibly have made that kind of money, not when he didn't have a drachma to his name."

Outraged, Stella cried, "Where did he come up with such a ludicrous accusation?"

"I don't know."

Stella rubbed her temple where she felt an ache. "Theo has been out of the country for six years working his head off to build a successful career. Nikos is only making wild accusations because his own business plans didn't turn out to be successful."

"I'm sure jealousy enters into it. Stasio's been trying to reason with him, but Nikos insists he's going to have Theo investigated."

"What? That's crazy."

"You're right. Poor Renate has no influence over him right now. She wants to go back to Switzerland, but he won't hear of it. He won't even talk to me, but then he never did like me so that's no news."

Nikos had never approved of Rachel, though he'd had to pretend to get along with her because she was Stasio's wife. At this point Stella feared the worst. "Nikos isn't behaving rationally right now. You should have seen him. He didn't care that Ari and Dax were watching."

"How awful. Listen…when Stasio comes up to bed, I'll tell him you're waiting for his call. He'll be relieved you're available to talk."

"Okay. Love you, Rachel. Take care of yourself."

"Ditto."

They hung up before she realized she hadn't even asked her sister-in-law about her nausea. She eased herself down under the covers and waited for Stasio's call, but he didn't phone for another half hour. It was after midnight when she finally said hello to him.

"I'm so sorry you had to find out about Theo through Nikos. I wanted to handle this myself before I told you."

"I understand. My whole concern is for you."

"I know that. The point is, Theo is back in Greece and he wants to be a father to Ari. He's not asking for anything else. I have to tell you he's done nothing but be wonderful to Ari and me. As I told Rachel, he said he'd been accosted before he could meet me at the church that night, and then he could never find me again.

"He sent me a letter that was sent back to him saying addressee unknown. I saw it with my own eyes. According to him someone tried to destroy our love. I…I believe him, Stasio, even though he hasn't told me everything."

"Did you read what the letter said?"

She shivered. "No. I was too angry at the time, but while I'm on St. Thomas, I'll ask him to let me see it."

"When are you going there again?"

"Tomorrow. I'll stay in touch with you while we're gone. As for Nikos, please don't tell him where I am." Stella had made a decision. "After our vacation I'm going to find a new place to live. As long as Nikos continues to stay at the villa when he comes to Athens, it's not a place I want to be."

After they got back from their vacation, if her brother ever came near her or Ari or Theo again with threats of any kind, then she'd call Costas, their family attorney, and have a restraining order put on him.

"Stella…you have every right to be upset. Before things go any further, let's meet in the morning on Andros to talk."

"You mean with Nikos?"

"Yes. It can't hurt anything. If you include him, he'll see you've forgiven him for his outburst on St. Thomas. When he learns that Theo wants to be a father to his son, he'll settle down enough to be more reasonable."

"No he won't, Stasio. He's never fully accepted Ari. Knowing Theo is back in Ari's life is only going to make him more unpleasant to be around. I won't let him hurt my son."

"I'll try to reason with him one more time."

"Thank you for that. I love you, Stasio."

"I love you, too. If Theo is all the things you believe he is and he can make Ari happy, then I couldn't ask more for you. When you never developed an interest in another man, I prayed Theo might come back to you."

Her eyes smarted. The kisses they'd exchanged over the last few days might have rocked her to the foundations, but these were still early days in their tentative relationship. "I…I'm not sure about that, but I do know he wants to father Ari from now on."

"Six years is a long time to be out of his life," Stasio murmured, "but it's never too late. A boy needs his own father if he's lucky enough to have him."

Stasio was talking about their father of course. Her brother was a saint. To have his blessing was all that mattered to Stella. Now that he knew everything, she felt free and couldn't wait to see Theo tomorrow.

"Kyrie Pantheras?"

Theo was on an overseas call. "What is it?" he asked his secretary.

"There's a courier from the court here with a summons. You have to sign for it."

He'd been expecting it. Nikos Athas hadn't wasted any time. "Send him in."

Theo made his excuses to the other man on the phone and hung up. In a minute the courier entered his office. Theo walked over to him. "I understand you have a summons for me?"

"Yes. If you'll sign and date it, please."

After he'd written his signature, he was given the envelope. Theo closed the door and walked over to the window to open the document.

Pantheras *vs* Athas.

Now that Nikos was back in the picture, Theo had tripled the security on himself, his family, not to mention Stella and Ari. Nikos had tried to destroy them once before. It could happen again. He wouldn't put anything past him and wasn't about to take any chances.

Plaintiff Nikos Athas seeks a restraining order against Defendant Theo Pantheras who has proved to be a threat to Plaintiff's sister, Stella Athas, and her son, Ari. You are hereby summoned to appear before the court at nine a.m., Wednesday, June 15, to answer to charges of manipulation and coercion with intent to harm. Failure to comply will result in your arrest.

Nikos must have been born with a twisted mind.

This summons was what the six years of hard work, sacrifice and preparation had all been about. Theo was more than ready to take on Stella's brother. Since being with her again, heaven knew he hadn't wanted it to come to this, but after bumping into Nikos on St. Thomas, their chance meeting had escalated the situation to a white-hot point.

Theo tapped the paper against his cheek. Stasio Athas's name wasn't on the suit. At this point he began to think he'd been totally wrong about Stella's oldest brother. Stasio had been the one to take her to New York and look after her. He'd been the one to come to Ari's rescue when he and Rachel had been kidnapped. Stella loved Stasio.

He moved over to his desk and phoned Nestor. "I just received a summons from Nikos Athas out of Costas Paulos's office. Who is he?"

"The Athas family attorney. Read me what it says."

After Theo complied, Nestor grunted. "I'll answer it and be in touch with you."

"Thank you. As you know, I don't want a court fight. Do everything you can to prevent it."

"That may not be possible. Costas is one of the best there is and could hold sway over the judge."

"When I made inquiries, I was told you were one of the best, but whatever happens, keep me posted. I'll be on vacation for the next ten days."

"Enjoy yourself. You deserve it."

"Thanks, Nestor."

With that out of the way, Theo couldn't wait to leave the office. He had plans for the three of them, plans he was praying would change his entire life.

\* \* \*

The resort's swimming pool resembled an aqua-blue lake. At one end was the giant slide Theo had told the boys about. Ari had been going down it all afternoon. Stella had taken quite a few turns herself and was worn-out. The hike to the top of the slide provided a work out all its own.

Theo never seemed to tire. He and Ari had thought up a dozen different ways to descend. Her boy was in heaven. If she didn't miss her guess, Theo was, too.

Ari ran over to the stairs. "I'm coming down on my stomach next time, Papa!"

Theo grinned. "Be sure and keep your head up. I'm waiting for you!"

"This is the last one for today, honey," Stella called to him from the sun lounger. "You and your father have your star-gazing class tonight. You need to eat dinner before you go."

"Oh, yeah. I forgot."

As he scrambled up the steps, Stella's gaze drifted to Theo who stood at the bottom of the serpentine slide to watch for him. Every female in the vicinity had their eyes on him, but Theo appeared oblivious. He and Ari were having too much fun.

Stella had brought out a book to read, but she kept looking at the same page over and over again because all she'd done was stare at the dark-haired male no other man compared to. One day Ari would grow up to be every bit as gorgeous and arresting. It gave her a thrill to know she was with Theo, that Ari was their son.

Several females cast her an envious glance. One woman who'd walked over to this part of the pool in a minuscule bikini made a play for him, engaging him in conversation. Stella felt so territorial she wanted to push her into the water, but of course she didn't do it. For one thing, Theo would know without a doubt her attraction to him had reached a dangerously strong level.

*Close your eyes, Stella. Don't look at him.*

Ari's life had become complete with the advent of his father's vital presence. His unqualified show of love for their son should be enough for Stella. Theo's private life was something else again.

They'd been here four days already. Once this vacation was over, she would get an apartment in the same neighborhood and life would get back to a new kind of normalcy. She'd go back to her work. So would he. Theo had talked about wanting a relationship with her, but they needed to go slowly.

In the meantime she had to put up with other women eyeing him. His kind of charisma brought the females running, just like the one with the tanned body and flowing blond hair still talking to him while he watched for Ari.

Since Theo seemed to be enjoying the attention, Stella decided she'd watched the spectacle long enough. After putting the book in her bag, she slipped on her beach coverup and headed inside the hotel where she wouldn't have to undergo more torture.

Certain things had changed since six years ago when Theo had never done anything to make her jealous. But that was when they'd been young lovers hiding from their families in order to be together. Everything was different now.

As she let herself in the room adjoining Theo's penthouse suite, a shaft of pain robbed her of breath because a part of her didn't want things to be different. In her heart of hearts she longed to be in his arms again. She ached for that fulfillment he'd brought to her life while they'd shut out the rest of the world.

But you could never go back. She didn't want to revisit all the pain that followed after he'd disappeared. Somehow she had to learn to survive with him back in Ari's life, but maybe not hers! Much to Ari's chagrin this special time with him on St. Thomas wouldn't last much longer, but it would be the very best antidote for the illness slowly killing her.

With tears threatening, she hurried into her room with the intention of showering, but all of a sudden Theo burst in through the adjoining door. Ari ran in behind him and disappeared into the bathroom.

"How come you didn't wait for us?" was the first question out of his mouth.

Stella was surprised he'd even noticed. "You two were having such a great time, I didn't know how long you'd be."

She heard him curse before he said, "You and I need to talk." He sounded angry.

"What's wrong?"

"How would you have felt if you'd turned around and discovered I was missing."

"It's not the same thing, Theo. You were talking to that woman. I didn't know if it was about business or not so I decided not to disturb you."

"That woman was a total stranger to me. When she invited me to a party, I told her I was married and my wife was right over there. Except that you weren't anywhere in sight."

"I'm sorry. I don't know what else to say."

"It upset Ari, too."

By now her heart was thundering unmercifully. "I had no idea."

"Next time give me a thought before you bolt." In the next breath he was gone.

"Mom?"

She swung around to see Ari with a towel wrapped around him. "Yes?"

"I thought you liked daddy."

Stella reeled. "You *know* I do. I've already told you that."

"But you don't love him like you used to, huh?"

His question trapped her. No matter how she answered it, Ari would internalize it and eventually tell Theo. "For now, why don't we concentrate on you and your father."

"I wish we could stay here forever."

Unable to resist, she kissed his cheek. "I've never seen you have so much fun before."

His dark eyes shone. "I love him."

"He loves you."

"I know. He's going to take us sailing tomorrow. We're going to stay out overnight and the next day we're going to fish."

"That'll be exciting for you."

"But you'll be with us."

"I don't think so, honey. Your father wants some private time with you. Think of all the years you've both missed."

His cute face crumpled. "Daddy says we won't go if you don't come."

Was Theo worried that Ari might get frightened without her there? If he could have heard his son just now, he'd know the bond between them was so strong, he had nothing to fear in that regard. After they came back from class she would ask Theo about it and reassure him if necessary.

"I'll talk to him later."

"We're going to eat dinner in his room. Come on. You can talk to him right now."

"Not yet. I have to shower first."

A few minutes later Stella rushed back into the bedroom and dressed in a pair of tan slacks and a print top in various shades of earth tones. She'd picked up a darker tan over the past few days. The new lipstick she'd purchased accentuated it. For the first time in years she felt as if she was on a real vacation with nothing to do but eat, sleep and play. She never wanted it to end.

In the past they'd always had to hide from everyone. Yet even after he'd disappeared, she'd never felt free. There was a gloom Nikos brought with him that had always darkened her world, but with Theo she felt free to be herself and Ari was a totally different child.

The more she thought about it, the more she was determined that as soon as they returned to Athens, she would start looking for another place to live. Stasio and his family preferred living on Andros. That left Nikos who could take over the family villa where he'd grown up. It would make him feel in charge. Maybe that's what he needed.

When she walked into Theo's suite, he captured her gaze. They both studied each other. "You look beautiful."

"Thank you."

"In truth you're the most beautiful woman at this resort. I can't believe how lucky I am."

She tried to stifle her gasp of surprise, but she couldn't suppress the surge of pleasure that curled through her body. Since it was Theo, he'd already noticed the signs, like the fact that right now her breathing had grown shallow just being this close to him.

He could read all the little clues that meant she was so aware of him, she was jittery. Of course she wasn't fooling anyone, especially not him, but it was a game she had to play for self-preservation.

"I'm lucky to be with two such handsome men."

"Am I handsome?" Ari wanted to know.

"Yes, just like your father," she blurted before realizing what she'd just said. Theo simply smiled at her.

Stella looked away. "Um, this looks good." She sat down next to Ari where Theo served them a light dinner from the cart sent up from the kitchen. So far they'd been eating all their meals in his room. She loved the intimacy, like they were a real family.

Theo eyed her for a long moment, seeming to assess her until she felt exposed. Her heart did a little kick she couldn't control. "Did Ari tell you my plans for the next few days?"

"Yes. We were just talking about it." If they all went sailing overnight, they'd be away from her brother's long reach a little longer. Without hesitation she said, "I can't think of anything I'd rather do."

"Hooray!" Ari cried.

There was a look in Theo's dark eyes that told her he was pleasantly surprised. "In that case I'd like to leave early in the morning."

"We'll be ready. While you're at class, I'll pack."

"I'll see the galley is stocked with food. That was a luxury I couldn't provide when we used to go rowing. Remember?"

"I didn't know you went rowing with Daddy."

Stella almost choked on the lamb she was eating. "Sometimes we did." Ari had been conceived on one of those outings.

"Was it fun?"

Theo's jet-black gaze shot to hers. "How would *you* describe it?" he asked her in his deep voice.

She couldn't meet his eyes. "As I recall, it was a lot of hard work."

"But the end justified the means every time."

*Theo...*

Unable to sit there any longer, she got up from the table. "I think I'll get started on that packing. Enjoy your class and come back safely."

Stella couldn't get out of his room fast enough.

Two nights later Stella stood at the bow of the sailboat, gazing at the view.

"That's a sunset you don't see very often." Theo had come up behind her.

"It's glorious." She'd been marveling over a golden orange sky slowly fading into pink. He ran his hands up her arms, kissing the side of her neck. "Wh-where's Ari?" When Theo came up on her like that, she couldn't even talk clearly.

"In the galley finishing his ice cream. Why do you think I stole up here for a moment?" His hands caressed her shoulders.

"No, Theo," she cried, "this isn't the time—" But he wasn't listening to her.

"You're wrong. It's the perfect time. Before I went away, you were my whole life." He turned her around to face him. "Since I've been back, I've discovered you still are. *Agape mou,*" he whispered, finding her mouth,

avidly kissing her lips apart. "I need to taste your sweetness again."

His hunger for her made her forget everything else. All
she knew was that his mouth set her on fire and she
couldn't stop what was happening. As his passion grew,
she was engulfed in his arms, craving his touch. There was
no one in the world who could make her feel the way Theo
did. Her need to merge with him was overpowering.

He finally lifted his head enough to look into her
eyes. "I can't believe that when I flew to New York, you
were there, too, having our baby. I should have been
there for you." She heard tears in his voice. "We were
robbed of our lives for a long time. Now that we're back
together, I need this more than ever. Tell me you feel the
same way…."

For a dizzying moment she felt their bodies meld. The
chemistry between them had always been volatile. Right
now it was as if they'd never been apart. "Obviously I'm
not immune to you, Theo," she confessed on a little
moan of surrender, "but having told you that, it changes
nothing. We're not young kids anymore."

"No. We're a man and woman who've never been
able to stay away from each other."

She searched his eyes. "There are things we have to
talk about."

"I agree, but let's enjoy the rest of our trip first. This
is heaven for me. I want to make it last as long as
possible. Don't you?"

"Of course," she admitted, "but—"

"Do you trust me?"

She felt him probing deep into her soul. "Yes.
Otherwise I wouldn't be here."

"That's all I needed to hear."

Once again his mouth fused with hers. This was ecstasy. His lips roved over her face, capturing each feature. As she sought his mouth helplessly, she heard a sound behind them.

"What kind of fish do you think we'll catch tomorrow?"

While she tore her lips away and eased out of Theo's arms, he turned to Ari. "Probably some sea bass. It's very tasty. If they're not biting, then we'll do some snorkeling."

"Will we see a lot of things?"

"I'll take us to a spot where the water's so clean and pure, you won't believe what's swimming underneath."

"Will it be scary?"

"Not where we're going. Besides, your mom and I will be right there with you."

"Yeah."

"Now that we've dropped anchor for the night, come on and help me put the boat to bed."

"A boat doesn't go to bed, Papa."

"Sure it does. It's tired after working hard all day." Ari giggled. No one was more exciting to be with than Theo. "We have to clean up any messes, fasten down anything loose, turn out lights. There's a lot of stuff."

"Will we be able to fish as soon as we wake up?"

"Yes, but it'll be foggy so we'll throw out our lines and see what we can catch until the sun burns it off."

"How did you learn to fish?"

"My father taught me and my brothers. We had to go out very early to catch enough for my mother to cook."

"You mean for breakfast?"

"No. She used fish to make the food we sold at the taverna."

"But what if you didn't catch any?"

"That happened a lot."

"Then what did you do?"

"We had to go to the meat shops and wait for them to sell us the meat parts for a cheap price nobody wanted."

"You mean like brains and liver and stuff?"

"That's right."

"Did we eat brains at the taverna the other day?"

Theo roared with laughter. "No. For you she prepared the very best food."

"It was yummy."

Stella's heart swelled with emotion as she gathered Ari's damp towels and sandals and listened to them talk. For one six-year-old boy, he left a lot of items around, but she didn't care. Theo was telling her son things she hadn't known, not during all the time she'd spent with him.

"Papa? I'd like to live on this sailboat."

She chuckled along with Theo. Ari loved everything they did because he was with his father.

"Shall we do it? Shall we just sail off to wherever we want?"

"Could we?"

"Yes, but I think you'd start to miss your friends and school."

"Did you like school?"

"For the most part."

"I like recess the best."

"So did I. You must be my son."

"I am!" At that remark, Theo threw back his head and laughed that deep, rich laugh Stella loved to hear. "I wish Mom and I could live with you."

"I'd love it," Theo answered without hesitation. His narrowed gaze captured hers. "How about *you*, Stella?"

Her heart thudded in her chest. He didn't play fair

asking her a loaded question like that in front of their son. "Are you being serious?" She'd decided it was his turn to be put on the spot.

There was a strange tension between them. He finally said, "So serious that I'd like to discuss it further after we turn in."

Staggered by his response, Stella left the deck and hurried below. She needed to gather her wits and headed straight to the galley to finish cleaning up. The two of them followed a few minutes later.

There were two bedrooms, one with a double bed and another with two bunk beds. She would have slept with Ari, but Theo insisted she have the big bed because the men were on an adventure.

After kissing Ari good-night, Stella brushed her teeth and changed into a pair of navy-blue tailored pajamas. Turning on the reading lamp, she sat up in bed and pulled out the book she'd tried to read at the pool. It was a spy novel written by an author she liked.

To her dismay she couldn't get into it tonight, either. When Theo entered the room dressed in a pair of sweats and a T-shirt, her heart thumped so hard, it hurt. In the semidarkness his striking masculine features stood out. Disturbed at the appealing sight of him, she pretended to keep reading.

In the next instant he came to sit down beside her and plucked it out of her hands. Then he got on the bed and stretched out next to her with one elbow propped. She felt his eyes study her with toe-curling intimacy. "You could have no comprehension of how gorgeous you look tonight."

She could hardly swallow. "Thank you."

"After I went to New York, there were nights when

I thought I'd die if I couldn't have you. I couldn't fathom that you'd stopped loving me."

Stella averted her eyes. "Then you have some comprehension of how I felt. It took raising Ari to help me deal with the pain."

He took a shuddering breath. "I threw myself into work. I had three jobs, one with a well-to-do Greek café owner who was a boyhood friend of my grandfather's. He told me that if I wanted to make real money, I should study the real estate listings. There were properties I could buy without a down payment. The trick was to fix one up and then sell it for as much as I could.

"I thought he was crazy, but I took his advice. You wouldn't believe how fast I started making money. He told me where to put it. Some of it went to high-risk investments that paid off. I sent money home and started planning my return. One of my goals was to find you and make you tell me face-to-face what happened."

She stirred restlessly on the bed before flicking him a glance. "I was the opposite. It was such a nightmare, I hoped I'd never see you again."

Theo grimaced. "My letter must have come as a shock."

"I fainted, but Iola caught me so I didn't crack my head open on the floor." The compassion in his eyes was too much. She looked away again.

"I'm sorry, Stella. After driving past the villa and seeing you, I didn't know how else to make contact."

She moistened her lips. "No matter how it was done, it was like finding out you'd come back from the dead."

"I was told you'd gotten rid of our child."

"Theo—"

"To see Ari skipping along with you almost sent me

into cardiac arrest. To think the whole time in New York, I believed—"

"That I'd ended my pregnancy?" she cut in on him. "How you must have despised me."

His body stiffened with remembered pain. "I was riddled with rage until I saw Ari. Then I was plunged into another kind of fury because you'd kept him from me."

After taking a deep breath she said, "Who did this to us?"

"It doesn't matter anymore." He leaned over her. "In the beginning I tried to despise you, but I couldn't. I fell in love with you a long time ago, Stella. That's never going to change. Marry me, sweetheart. I can't go on without you."

She let out a little moan as he began kissing her, sweeping her away. "I never stopped loving you, either. You're my whole life!"

"Did you just say yes?"

"You *know* I did," she cried. "I love you, I love you, Theo. I want to be your wife as soon as possible."

"Stella—" came his exultant cry. "Let me love you tonight. Really love you."

The feel of his mouth brought her such rapture, she'd become a trembling mass of need. Over and over she cried out his name. His powerful legs entwined with hers, reminding her of those other times when they'd given in to their desire.

"Papa?"

They both groaned.

"When are you coming back to bed?"

"Don't tell him yet," she whispered. "Let's wait until we know all our plans."

"Agreed." Theo kissed her throat before rolling away from her. "I thought you were asleep, sport."

"I had a nightmare."

"Oh, honey," Stella said. "Come on up here." Ari scrambled on the bed between them. "What was it about?"

"A shark. It was trying to catch me."

"Well, you stay right here with us. We'll keep you safe."

She felt Theo's fingers creep into her hair, tantalizing her. He'd expected her to urge Ari back to bed so they could take up where they'd left off, but it wouldn't be a good idea for several reasons. The main one was snuggled up against them happy as a new puppy, his nightmare forgotten.

"Good night, everyone."

"Good night, Mom. Good night, Papa."

Theo squeezed her shoulder. "Good night, Mom. Good night, son."

"Mommy's not your mom."

More deep laughter reverberated in the room. It was the last thing she remembered before falling asleep.

By the time their vacation was over, Stella felt like they were a family. She could have stayed there forever playing with and loving the two men she adored. The thought of going back to work made her groan. That was how transported she'd been.

"What was that sigh all about?" Theo was so tuned in to her feelings, they could read each other's minds.

"How much I don't want this to be over." The three of them were carrying their bags to the helicopter.

He caught her around the waist. "It's not going to be. You and I need more time together. Hire a temp to help Keiko for another week. Someone in the office will want the opportunity."

Another week with Theo? She almost stumbled in her excitement. "I'll see what I can arrange."

Before long they flew back to civilization. When the helicopter landed on top of his office building, Stella rebelled. For a moment she had the premonition that now he'd asked her to marry him, this fragile new world they'd been building was going to explode by an unseen force and they'd never be able to pick up the pieces.

As Theo helped her out of the helicopter she whispered, "Do you still have that letter? I'm ready to read it."

His black eyes ignited like hot coals. He pressed a hungry kiss to her mouth. "It's in my office."

"Will you get it for me before you drive me and Ari home?"

"I'll do it right now and join you at the limo." He ruffled Ari's hair. "See you in a minute."

# CHAPTER EIGHT

THEO made a detour to his suite. There was a message waiting for him. Nestor had talked to the judge, but there was no budging him. The show-cause hearing was going ahead as planned for the day after tomorrow.

He closed his eyes tightly, imagining Stella's reaction. After asking her to marry him, he'd do anything to protect her from being hurt, but it was all going to come out, and he was terrified what it would do to her.

The letter was in his drawer. He put it in his pocket and left his office, catching up to them out in front of the building. The second he climbed in the back next to Stella, Ari said, "I wish we didn't have to go home. I love fishing."

"So do I, son. After our astronomy class has ended, we'll do it again. I know a place in the mountains where we can camp out and fish the stream. Leandros and his papa love to fish, too. Maybe the four of us could go. Would you like that?"

"I'd love it."

That was one of the things he loved most about Ari. His constant enthusiasm. Stella had been right. Their son was the brightest, sweetest boy in the world. They were both his life!

Too soon the limo drove up in front of the villa, bringing their trip to an end.

"See you tomorrow, Papa." Ari gave him a big kiss and climbed out first. Taking advantage of the moment, Theo drew the letter from his pocket and put it in her purse lying next to her on the seat.

He reached for her hand and kissed the palm. "Call Keiko and make those arrangements. I have more plans for us."

She nodded. "I'll let you know tomorrow."

"Stella—" He cupped her face to kiss her one more time. It wasn't long enough or deep enough.

"Come on, Mom."

Theo reluctantly let her go.

"Good night." She got out of the car, leaving him with an ache that was never going to go away.

He watched her rush up the steps to join Ari. Once they were safely inside, he told the chauffeur to take him back to the office. Theo knew he wouldn't be able to sleep, so he might as well get some work done.

A time bomb was ticking. Before long it was going to go off. There had to be a way to help Stella when the time came, but his greatest fear was that she would go into shock. When he thought about one of his own brothers having the capacity to betray him to that degree, he couldn't imagine it.

One thing and one thing only was helping him to hold on to his sanity tonight. To his everlasting gratitude, he had Ari, his greatest ally and link to Stella. Ari always pulled through for him.

What a wonderful son. His joy. That's because he had a mother like Stella. On this trip Theo found out he needed them like he needed air to breathe. If the crisis that was coming was too much for her, he might never be able to reach her again in the same way.

This trip had drawn them so close together, the thought of anything destroying what they had now was killing him. He buried his face in his hands.

Iola took one look at Ari and threw up her hands. "You've turned into a lobster!"

"Lobster…" Ari roared with laughter. "Guess what? I caught two sea bass!"

"How big were they?"

"This long." He demonstrated.

"Good for you! Did you eat them?"

"Yes. Papa's the best cook just like my grandma. The fish was yummy, wasn't it, Mommy."

"Delicious." On their trip she'd discovered Theo had many hidden skills.

"Are you hungry now?"

"No. We're ready for bed," Stella declared. "If he's going to play with Dax in the morning, he needs his sleep. Run on up, honey, and get your bath. I'll be there in a minute to tuck you in."

"Okay."

As he darted up the stairs, she turned to Iola. "How are you?"

"I'm fine now that you've come home so happy. You're in love again."

Stella nodded. "Theo's even more wonderful than he was before."

"He's a man."

"Yes. He's my life and Ari's." She kissed Iola's cheek. "See you in the morning."

Once in her room, she couldn't wait to read the letter.

Her hands trembled as she got it out of her purse. When he'd given it to her on Andros, she'd thrown it back at him. At the time, her state of mind wouldn't allow him inside her head. Now he filled her whole heart and soul.

She sank down on the side of her bed, dying to find out what he'd written. Taking as much care as possible, she opened the sealed envelope and pulled out the short, one-page letter.

Agape Mou,
Something terrible has happened to me. That's why I couldn't come inside the church to get you. I'm in Salamis Hospital, room 434W. Spiro is writing this letter for me because I can't use my hands yet.

Find a way to leave the villa and come to me as fast as you can, sweetheart. My family's going to let you stay with us until I'm better, then we'll get married and find a place of our own.

I love you, Stella. I love our baby.
Come soon. I need you.
Theo.

Stella moaned.

"Kyrie Pantheras?"
"Yes?"
"Stella Athas is here to see you."
Excitement charged his body. "Tell her to come in." He threw down his pen and hurried around the desk to greet her. This morning she was wearing a stunning cocoa-colored silk blouse with pleated pants in a café-au-lait tone.

She looked good enough to eat. Her velvety brown

eyes sought his with a new eagerness. She must have read his letter or she wouldn't have that expectant look on her face.

"Am I disturbing you?"

"Yes," he whispered in a husky tone and reached for her, sliding his hands up and down her arms. "In all the ways only you can do." He could tell she was out of breath. "Did you work things out with Keiko?"

She nodded.

"Anything else you want to tell me?"

"Yes. It's about us. Weeks ago you asked me to accept you on faith. Last night on the boat you asked me to marry you. It's what I want, what Ari wants. That's what I've come here to say and I want us to tell Ari today."

"Stella," he cried. "I prayed that was why you'd come. Now that you're here, I don't intend to waste another second."

He lowered his mouth to the lush moistness of hers, leaving her no escape. They began devouring each other with a fervency that transported both of them back in time to halcyon days when nothing mattered but to be together communicating like this.

His body trembled with desire while they clung in such a tight embrace, there was no space between them. He couldn't believe it. She was giving him everything. It was as if a light had been turned on. Theo couldn't get enough of her as their kisses grew more breathless and sensual.

"I'm in love with you, Stella," he cried into her hair.

Her gasp of ecstasy thrilled him. She burrowed her face in his neck. "I'll love you forever, Theo. I couldn't get through life without you now."

To hear those words caused the blood to sing in his ears. "Do you think I could?" His euphoria made him forget everything except the wonder of holding and kissing her until he was delirious with longings that needed assuagement soon. They were already in deep trouble.

"Kyrie Pantheras? You asked me to buzz you when it was ten to twelve."

Stella's moan of protest was as loud as his.

"Thank you."

He drank from her mouth one more time before putting her away from. Her eyes were glazed from desire. She swayed in place.

"Only Ari could force me to let you go at a time like this."

She kissed his hands. "Let's go pick him up together. I can't wait to tell him our news. He'll be so happy." Her gaze played over him with so much love he felt like he was drowning.

Theo pressed his lips to her palms. "Neither of you could want it as much as I do. After we get him, I'm taking you both to my house on Salamis. While we have lunch there, we'll tell him it will be our home. I want to marry you right away. Will you mind living on the island?"

Her brows formed a delicate frown line. "How can you ask me that?"

"Because you've lived in the heart of Athens all your life."

"As long as I'm with you, I don't care where I live. We used to talk about the house we would have right on the beach one day. It was my dream. Have you forgotten?"

He caught her face between his hands. "There isn't one second of our lives I haven't lived over and over until it has driven me mad. I'm hardly going to forget the plans we made." After kissing her with refined savagery, he wheeled away from her to gather his suit jacket and the phone.

Together they rode the private elevator to the car park where his limo was waiting. En route to Dax's house he held her on his lap and kissed her senseless. For a little while he felt like a teenager again, crazy in love with Stella Athas, the most gorgeous girl in the world.

"We've got to stop doing this before we get there, Theo. Ari's going to know what we've been up to."

He chuckled. "Our son knows exactly what's been going on with us from day one." She slid off his lap and sat across from him to brush her hair. "I love the taste of your lipstick by the way. You can lay it on me anytime."

"Behave, Theo."

"I don't want to. Besides, you don't want me to."

"That's beside the point," she said while she applied a fresh coat to her lips.

"Are you as happy as I am?"

She shot him a glance that enveloped him in love. "I'm so happy I'm in pain. The kind that's never going to go away."

"We can be married in three weeks, Stella. I'll arrange it with Hektor."

Three weeks without being married sounded like an eternity. While Stella was wondering how she would last until then, the limo turned into Dax's driveway. The boys were out in front throwing a ball. Ari waved goodbye to his friend and ran toward them.

"Mom!" He climbed inside next to Theo. "I didn't know you were coming with Papa. This is great!"

"Your mother and I have a plan. I'll tell the driver to run us to your house. Both of you grab some clothes for a sleepover and we'll spend the night at my house. Though you've seen it, your mother hasn't."

"Goody! Will we go to class from there?"

Theo nodded. "Tell me what you and Dax did this morning."

Stella scarcely listened. Too much excitement over the news they had to tell Ari made her restless. Not only that, she couldn't wait to see Theo's house.

While they were at class, she had a wedding to plan. Rachel would help her. She'd include Elani, too. In fact she'd call them both tonight. It would be a joyous time for all of them.

"Stella?" Theo whispered. "What's going on inside that lovely head of yours?" She blinked to realize they were in front of the villa.

"Ari's gone in to get his things."

"I need to get mine, too."

"Just a minute." He pressed a deep kiss to her mouth. "Tell me you're not having second thoughts. I couldn't handle it."

"Hush, Theo." She kissed him back passionately. "Actually I was thinking of Rachel and how excited she'll be to help me plan our wedding."

"I'm looking forward to meeting her."

"You'll love her."

He kissed her temple. "Do you want me to come in while you get your things?"

"No. It'll only take me a minute."

"Hurry!"

"I promise."

He helped her out. She passed Ari in the foyer with his backpack. "I'll be right out, honey." All she needed were some toiletries, a change of clothes and a nightgown.

While she was putting everything in her overnight bag, Iola came in her bedroom. "Where are you going?"

She closed the lid. "To Theo's. I'm not sure when we'll be home. It might be a few days."

"Are you sure you know what you're doing?"

"Absolutely. Iola, you might as well know first. We're back together for good. In fact we're getting married in three weeks."

Her eyes filled with tears before she broke down with happy sobs. Stella gave her a hug. "You'll have to help me with the wedding plans."

Iola finally pulled herself together. "Before I forget, Rachel wants you to call her right away. She says it's an emergency."

"Thanks for telling me. I'll phone her."

"Good."

After she walked out, Stella reached for her phone. She'd purposely turned off the ringer while she'd gone to Theo's office. Much as she'd like to put off this call, she couldn't, but with Ari and Theo outside waiting for her, she'd make this fast.

It barely started to ring when Rachel answered. "Stella?"

"Hi. What's wrong?"

"If you have to ask me that question, then you don't know."

Her heart picked up speed. "Know what?"

After a silence. "I hope you're sitting down."

Stella stood there unable to move. "If this is about Theo, I don't want to hear it."

"You have to hear it, Stella." She heard tears in Rachel's voice.

"Then tell me."

"Nikos has brought a full-blown lawsuit against Theo for misrepresenting who he is and taking advantage of you. The case is set for tomorrow morning. He expects the family to be there for support. I told him I wouldn't have anything to do with it. Stasio's in shock that Nikos has carried it this far."

"I am, too," she murmured. It meant Theo had been aware of the court date for some time now, but he'd never let on.

"Stella?"

"I have to go now."

"Are you all right?" Rachel sounded frantic.

"No. I have to talk to Theo. Tell Stasio I'll call him later."

She hung up feeling so ill she didn't know if she'd survive another second. For her brother to do this at the height of her happiness made him sound unbalanced. In a panic, she rushed downstairs and out the front entrance to the car.

Theo opened the limo door and gave her a squeeze around the waist. "We thought you were never coming."

Avoiding his eyes she said, "I had a phone call that detained me. Before we go anywhere, I need to talk to you alone."

She lowered her head to look at Ari. "Honey? There's something I have to discuss with your father in private. It will only take a minute. Would you mind running inside the house? I'll let you know when we're finished."

He could tell she was serious. His happy expression faded. "Okay." He slid out of the limo leaving his pack behind and raced up the porch steps into the house.

Stella climbed inside and sat opposite Theo. He sat

back, studying her features. She saw nothing but love in those dark eyes.

"Rachel just phoned me. I've been told Nikos has brought a lawsuit against you and you have to appear in court tomorrow. Is it true?"

She thought he paled. "Yes."

"Why didn't you tell me?"

"Because I wanted to put the past behind us."

"I don't understand my brother. There's something really wrong with him."

"Let me worry about it."

"How can you be so calm? Were you planning to go to court without me?"

"Yes. I don't want you there."

"I've just told you I'll marry you. You think I'd let you walk into a courtroom alone after what we've been through in the last six years?"

"You can't come, Stella. I won't let you. The court session shouldn't take long. I'll be back soon enough."

Stella decided not to argue with him. After he left for court, she'd take Ari to Dax's house and slip into the courtroom. Theo wouldn't be able to do anything about it then.

"All right."

He kissed her hard on the mouth. "I'll go in and get Ari now."


"Third district court is now in session. The Most Honorable Judge Antonias Christopheles presiding."

"You may be seated," the judge said, looking out at the crowd assembled.

Besides Theo's entire family, including Hecktor, half of the closed-session courtroom was filled with witnesses Nestor had lined up. The other half of the room was conspicuously empty. Nikos sat at the table with his attorney, but just as the judge began to speak, Stella slipped inside the back and sat down next to Stasio.

Theo hadn't wanted her anywhere near here, but there wasn't anything he could do about it now.

"There are several charges laid before the court this Wednesday, the eighteenth of June by Nikos Athas against Theo Pantheras for unduly manipulating and coercing Stella Athas against her will. Mr. Pantheras, in turn, has laid countercharges against Nikos Athas.

"The first is to ascertain if Nikos Athas intended to murder Theo Pantheras on July 6, six years ago.

"The second is to discover if he set fire to the Pantheras Taverna in Paloukia on the night of July 1.

"The third is to discover if he caused an accident to Spiro Pantheras while he was riding his motor scooter the night of June 27.

"The fourth is to learn if he threatened the lives of the Pantheras family on repeated occasions by telephone calls from June 2 until July 6."

"The fifth is to learn if he tried to bribe Theo Pantheras with ten thousand dollars to leave his sister alone."

With each count, Theo watched Stella's head drop a little lower. He'd warned her not to come. This part was going to devastate her.

"Mr. Paulos, if you'll make your opening statement, please."

Theo watched the burly-looking attorney take the floor. "Thank you, Your Honor. My client has been forced to respond to these totally false allegations without having been given adequate preparation time."

"I'm aware of that. However, may I remind you this

is only a show-cause hearing to determine if this case warrants a full jury trial. Please go ahead."

"Thank you." He cleared his throat. "Athas Shipping Lines is one of Greece's greatest resources. I don't need to tell the court of Nikos Athas's extraordinary talents as one of our Olympians. Their father filled one of the highest positions in our government.

"To think Nikos could perpetrate such crimes is beyond the imagination of this counsel and I dare say this country. I consider it a crime to waste this court's time, Your Honor. If opposing counsel can produce one shred of evidence to the contrary, then let him speak."

The judge nodded. "Mr. Georgeles? If you'll approach the bench."

Nestor patted Theo's arm before getting to his feet. "If Your Honor will look at Exhibit A, I'll ask the physician, Dr. Vlasius, who attended Mr. Pantheras in the E.R. at Salamis Hospital on the night of July 6 to explain. He's on the board there now."

"Step forward, Doctor, and be sworn in."

Once that was accomplished, Nestor began. "Dr. Vlasius, would you tell us about these X-rays, please."

"Certainly. These show the injuries to Mr. Theo Pantheras, the nineteen-year-old man brought in by his friends. When he was beaten up on his way home and left for dead, it revealed that the bones in his lower legs, arms and hands had been broken by a pipe. The type of weapon used has been corroborated by the police. His face was smashed in. He resided in the hospital six weeks while his bones healed and reconstructive surgery was done on his face and nose."

A feminine cry came from across the aisle. Stella's.

"Thank you, Dr. Vlasius. If you'd be seated, I'd like

to call on Damon Arabos, Theo's closest friend who brought him in to the hospital."

Again Theo could tell Stella was stunned to see him walk to the bench. He'd been Theo's sidekick through high school. He was a tease who'd made everyone laugh.

As soon as he was sworn in, Nestor began. "Did you witness this attack on him?"

"Only at the end."

"Did you recognize who did it?"

"There were five men bent over him. I got some of our friends and we started to attack them. They ran away and got in a van. One of our friends took down the license plate. The police traced it to a man who works at the docks for Athas Shipping Lines named Yanni Souvalis, but he suddenly didn't show up for work anymore."

"Thank you, Mr. Arabos. You may be seated. Now I'd like to call Alena Callas to the bench to be sworn in. She works at the telephone company in their records department and has gathered some evidence useful to this case which I've submitted under Exhibit B."

This was the part Theo had been waiting for. It was the paper trails that would bring Nikos down.

"Mrs. Callas, would you tell the court the nature of Exhibit B."

"Yes. These represent the phone logs of the dates between June 2 and July 6. Nine phone calls in all. They originated from the private phone of Mr. Nikos Athas. All calls were made to the Pantheras Taverna on Salamis Island."

"Were they long phone calls?"

"Each one was different, but none of them were longer than forty-five seconds."

"Thank you. You can be seated. I'd like to call Mr. Bion as my next witness."

"I object, Your Honor!" Mr. Paulos blurted.

"Objection overruled. I'm here to listen to the evidence. Please make it short, Mr. Georgeles."

"Yes, Your Honor."

Theo couldn't see Nikos's face. He was huddled behind the desk with his attorney.

"Mr. Bion? Please tell the court who you are."

"I'm the battalion commander for the Paloukia Fire Department."

"Were you witness to a fire at the Pantheras Taverna on the night of July 1?"

"Yes, sir. Of course, then I had just joined the department."

"Tell us what you discovered at the fire?"

"It was an arson case. A chemical was used that the police traced to Athas Shipping Lines. Only a few companies use it."

"So it could have come from another shipping line?"

"Not at that time, no."

"Thank you. You can be seated. I'd now like to call Mr. Spiro Pantheras to the stand."

Spiro winked at Theo on his way to the bench.

"Tell the court who you are, please."

"I'm Spiro Pantheras, Theo's older brother."

"I understand you met with an accident on your motor scooter on the night of June 27 near the taverna."

"That's correct."

"Can you tell us what happened."

"I was on my way home from the store when I heard a car rev behind me. I moved to the right to get out of the way, but it followed me and sideswiped me, knocking me off my scooter."

"Did you see the car?"

"Only the tail end of it before it rounded the corner. It was the latest model black Ferrari with local license plates."

"Were you hospitalized?"

"No, but because of the threatening phone calls to my parents at the *taverna*, I called the police to report it. You have a copy of the police case."

"Did anything happen as a result?"

"No."

"Thank you very much. You may step down." Nestor turned to the judge. "Your Honor? If you'll look at Exhibit C, I've provided a list of every new Ferrari sold within that twelve-month period in Athens. Two could be accounted for. One belonged to the deputy prime minister, the other to Nikos Athas. For my final witness today, I call Theo Pantheras to the stand."

This was it, but Theo felt no joy having to expose her brother this way in front of her. After he was sworn in, Nestor said, "Mr. Pantheras, please tell the court in your own words the happenings during that month leading to your hospitalization."

He took a deep breath and leveled his gaze on Stella. "I committed the crime of falling in love with Stella Athas when she was sixteen and I, eighteen. Her family didn't approve of me and we both knew it, so we had to be creative how we could be together.

"I knew Nikos Athas didn't like me, but I didn't realize he'd go so far as to harass me and my family so I'd stay away from her. One night he followed me home from church. On the way he offered me ten thousand dollars to get out of Stella's life and stay out.

"I told him what he could do with his money and took off. Later that week we received threatening phone calls from him, then the *taverna* was set on fire. After Spiro's accident I realized Nikos was serious. On the last phone call I received from him, he said that if I didn't break up with Stella, he would injure my parents until I didn't recognize them.

"I had to believe him, so I called Stella and told her we were getting married. I'd meet her at the church, but I was beaten up outside in the car park. It was clear Nikos wasn't about to let the Pantheras family merge with his on any level, not even to letting me claim my rights as a father.

"After I got out of the hospital, I left for New York to begin carving out a career for myself. Since then I've returned to Greece and have been with Stella and my son Ari."

Nestor smiled at Theo. "Thank you, Mr. Pantheras. You may step down." Theo went back to his seat behind the desk. "Your Honor, I turn the time back over to Mr. Paulos."

"Mr. Paulos?" the judge asked. "Do you wish to cross-examine?"

"Not at this time, Your Honor."

"What can he say?" Nestor whispered to Theo. "There is no rebuttal to the case we just presented. His case has fallen apart."

Theo agreed. Nikos had already hung himself.

"After hearing the proceedings of this case, I plan for this to go to a full jury trial which is set for September 13. Bail on Nikos Athas is set at ten million dollars. You will not be allowed to leave the country."

Nikos exploded. "You can't keep me here! I live in Switzerland!"

"One more outburst, Mr. Athas, and I'll have the sergeant-at-arms restrain you. This session is dismissed until September 13 at 9:00 a.m." He pounded his gavel and left the courtroom.

The family swarmed around Theo. This was a day they'd needed for closure. Everyone wept. When Theo eventually stood up to find Stella, he discovered she had gone. The emptiness in his heart threatened to swallow him whole. Charging her brother with attempted murder wasn't something easy to forgive. He would treasure the memories of the last few weeks with her and Ari, but they might be all he'd ever have.

# CHAPTER NINE

STELLA left the courtroom and raced to the villa ahead of everyone. "Iola?" she cried out the second she entered the house.

"I'm here." The housekeeper came running. "What's wrong?"

"Wait right here." She dashed up the stairs to get the letter Theo had sent her. When she came down again she said, "I'm going to show you something. I want you to think back very hard to the time when Theo didn't come to the church for me."

The older woman frowned. "I'll never forget it as long as I live."

No one would forget. "I want you to take a look at this envelope. Read everything on the front. The date is from six years ago." She handed it to her.

Iola studied it for an overly long moment without lifting her eyes.

Pure revelation flowed through Stella. "You recognize it, don't you."

Still no response.

"Is that your handwriting at the bottom that says addressee unknown?"

She shook her head violently.

"Do you know whose it is? This is important, Iola. I have to know the truth."

"I can't tell you."

"Why?"

"Because I will lose my job."

"What? That's impossible! You're a part of this family." Stella reached out and hugged her. "This is your home. Who told you that?"

She kept her head bowed. "Please don't make me tell you. I'm afraid."

"I can see that."

Stella put a hand over her own mouth, absolutely devastated to think Nikos had blackmailed her into keeping quiet about this. "Did more letters like this come to the house I don't know about?"

"I don't know," she muttered. In the next breath she handed Stella the letter before running down the hall toward the back of the villa.

Stella slowly walked into the salon and waited for the rest of the family to arrive. She'd arranged for Ari to stay with Dax until she came for him.

In a minute she heard footsteps in the foyer. Stasio's pained expression left nothing to the imagination as he entered the salon with Nikos, who'd gone somewhere mentally where she couldn't reach him.

His year-round tan had turned a sickly white. He'd been Stella's nemesis for years. Every truly unhappy moment in her life she could lay at his feet. Her own brother.

Poor Stasio. He'd been just as wounded by him, maybe more, because he was the big brother Nikos hated to love and loved to hate.

On impulse she reached for Nikos's hand. "I have something important to tell you, Nikos. Despite what you've done, I know in my heart Theo doesn't want to send you to prison. That wasn't his focus.

"When he came back to Greece and discovered he had a son, all he wanted was to fight for him and ultimately for me." Never had a woman had more evidence of a man's love.

She squeezed Nikos's hand to get a reaction from him. "Listen to me—I know he'll drop all the charges against you provided you do something for me."

He looked at her in torment.

"If he still wants me after this, we're going to be married. All he would like is peace from my family. He would like to be able to come and go with me and Ari and be treated kindly and fairly. That's all."

Stasio's eyes glistened with tears.

"But that's not all I want. Once upon a time you were a sweet boy, but something happened when you grew up. You'll have to promise me and Stasio that you'll get psychiatric help. You've needed it for years. It'll save your marriage. Renate really loves you, but she can't do it alone."

"It's too late for me," Nikos whispered in a tortured breath.

"No." Stasio sat forward. "It's never to late to change."

Stella patted his hand. "Look at Theo. He's back after six years ready to take up where we left off. He didn't think it was too late."

He shook his head. "I told the guys to rough him up, not kill him."

"I believe you. So does he."

"He has every right to hate my guts forever."

"Theo's not like that." Her voice trembled. "He has so much goodness in him you can't imagine."

The sobs started coming. Suddenly he got up from the couch and left the room. They could hear his anguish all the way to his suite down the hall.

Stasio moved over to sit by her. He put his big arms around her and rocked her against him. "Stella..." She heard every ounce of pain and love in his heart. They'd been through it all together. "When you and Theo work everything out, I want to have a long talk with him. He's a man like few others. No wonder no other guy ever measured up."

"I love him so terribly."

"I know. He's a lucky man to be loved by you. Go to him and put him out of his misery. He deserves every bit of happiness you can find together."

Since returning from court, Theo's family had sequestered him above the taverna. The women got food ready while he sat at the dining room table with his father and brothers. They'd closed the taverna for the day. It was like a holiday with the kids milling around, but the last thing he felt like doing was celebrating.

He kept reliving the court scene in his mind. With each damaging piece of evidence, Stella seemed to have shrunken inside herself a little more. No matter how he went over it in his mind, there hadn't been another way to do it.

If he'd called her on the phone after returning to Athens, and told her the truth right off, she would have hung up on him. There wouldn't have been a discussion. He would never have been able to meet Ari.

"Theo?" Dymas poured him a little wine. "She's going to forgive you."

Spiro nodded. "Give it time. You said she's always had to be careful around Nikos. When it sinks in and she realizes there wasn't any other way for you to handle things, she'll get in touch with you."

He sat back in the chair with his arms crossed. "I'd like to believe you, but I saw anguish on her face today. She has loved her family a lot longer than she has loved me. You know what they say. Blood is thicker than water." His gaze flicked to his family.

"Thank you all for being there for me today."

"As if we'd have been anywhere else." His father patted his arm. "You've suffered long enough. Today we saw justice done. I'm very proud of the great man you've become."

For his father to tell Theo that was something. He'd never said those words to him before. "Thank you, Papa, but I don't feel great. To destroy the woman I love in order to be with her and my son has brought me no joy."

"Nikos Athas destroyed himself without anyone's help, my boy."

"It's too bad the jury trial can't be sooner so this can all be over with."

"There isn't going to be one, Spiro." Theo shoved himself away from the table and got to his feet.

All three of them stared at him, waiting for an explanation.

"Tomorrow I'll tell Nestor I'm dropping the charges."

Dymas looked shocked. "After all you've done to get ready for it?"

"Yes. It's over."

"Nikos could still be dangerous."

"I've thought about that, Dymas. Nevertheless, today's court session is as far as I go. He's been exposed. Enough damage was done for Stella to know the true reason for what happened."

His father got to his feet and walked over to him. "How much does Ari know about any of this?"

"As far as I know, nothing. But today everything exploded. No doubt he'll learn all about it and totally despise me."

"No, Theo. You've won his love. He'll figure it out. Like Spiro said, give this time."

"You mean like another six years? Maybe then my son will be mature enough to acknowledge me again?" Theo was dying inside. "Papa? Will you tell Mama I couldn't stay. I have to leave."

He patted Theo's shoulder. "I understand. Where are you going to go?"

"I don't know. I need to be alone."

"Do you want to take a drive with me?"

"No, thank you, Papa. I have to be on my own." He felt like running until he dropped and the pain went away.

They walked to the top of the stairs. "I love you, Theo."

"I love you, too, Papa." He kissed his cheek before descending the steps leading to the restaurant below. He let himself out of the back of the *taverna* and locked the door before he started running in the direction of the beach.

Stella showered and changed into the white dress with the wide belt Theo seemed to like so much. Wherever he was, when she caught up to him she wanted to look her most beautiful for him.

After talking to Ari on the phone at Dax's house, she found out he hadn't heard from his father all day. It was after four right now. This had to be the first time Theo hadn't checked in with their son.

She grew even more apprehensive because they had their star-gazing class tonight. Theo could have gone anywhere after court. She wanted to believe he was with his family, but after what he'd lived through today, he was probably out of his mind in pain. Somehow she had to get through this and find him without alarming Ari.

Once she was ready, she said good-night to Stasio and slipped out the back door to her car. She'd told Ari to be waiting for her. When she eventually drove up to Dax's house, he came flying out the front door and jumped in the car.

"Where's Papa?"

She smothered the moan rising in her throat. "I think he's at the taverna with his family. I thought we'd drive there for dinner before you guys leave for class."

"He'll be glad. Papa's afraid you don't like his family."

Stella glanced at her son. "That's not true. I like them very much."

"He talks about you all the time and told me what you were like when he first met you. He said you were really shy. What does that mean?"

"That I didn't speak up and kind of hung back."

"Papa said that was his favorite thing about you. All the other girls...well, you know. They wanted to be with him, but he said that once he met you, that was it."

She was certain there'd been other women while he'd been in New York. He was too attractive and had too much drive to live like a monk, but he'd come back for her. It proved that whatever had gone on in his past, it hadn't kept him in the States. That was all that mattered to her.

"It's nice to hear."

"He wanted to know if you'd had boyfriends."

"What did you tell him?"

"That there'd been some, but you never let any of them come up to the family room or sleep over. Papa was pretty happy to hear that."

In spite of her fear that they wouldn't be able to find him, she chuckled. "I'm afraid when I met him, I never really looked at another man again."

"You love him like crazy, huh."

Her throat practically closed up with emotion. "Yes. How can you tell?"

"Because you're always smiling now."

"So are you. Let's go find him right now and surprise him."

They'd crossed over to Salamis Island. The traffic was horrendous with tourists and people driving home from work.

*Be there, Theo,* she cried. But when they came in sight of the taverna, she couldn't see his car. That didn't necessarily have to mean anything, but it still made her stomach clench.

She pulled up in front. Ari jumped right out. "I'll get him, Mom."

It was just as well he went inside alone. She didn't feel up to facing his family, not after what they'd all been through this morning in court.

Stella's brother had been the cause of all the pain their family had suffered. Nothing she could ever say or do would make up for what they'd had to endure. Whenever her mind remembered what the doctor had said in court about Theo's injuries, her heart broke all over again.

When Ari came back out, she had to dash the moisture off her cheeks so he wouldn't suspect anything was wrong.

"Grandpa said he was there earlier, but he left to go home."

"Then, that's where we'll go. Do you know where his house is from here? I've never seen it."

"Yeah. I'll show you how to get there. Take that road over there and follow it to the coast road."

Once they reached the other road, everything started to look familiar to her. With each kilometer she realized Ari was directing her toward a favorite area she hadn't seen in six years.

Before long Ari told her to turn into the driveway around the next curve. A gasp of surprise escaped her lips to see a lovely white villa on the stretch of beach where Theo used to take her in the rowboat.

"*This* is your father's house?"

"Yeah. It's so cool. It has a gym and an indoor pool. I can walk right out on the beach from my bedroom. We've set up the telescope on the porch and look at the stars. Dax wishes he lived here."

"I'll bet he does," her voice trembled.

They both got out of the car and walked past the flowering shrubs to the front entrance. "Papa gave me a key. Come on." He opened the door for them. She stepped inside a new, modern world of white with splashes of color on the walls and floors. So much light from the arched windows thrilled her to death.

"Papa?" he called out. "Mom and I are here! Where are you?" He raced around the house but couldn't find him. "He's probably gone for a walk. Let's go find him."

If he wasn't here, Stella didn't know what she would do. "That's a great idea. I'll take my shoes off."

"Me, too."

They left them inside the sliding doors off the family

room. She followed him outside. Steps led down from the deck to the sand. The evening air felt like velvet. Her eyes took in the ocean not thirty feet away.

The pristine beach was just as she remembered it from years ago. "Come on, Mom. This is the way Papa took me for a walk."

She ran to catch up to him. "There aren't any people around."

"This is his private beach. He said that when he was growing up, their family lived like sardines in a can." She laughed at the metaphor. "He decided that if he ever made enough money, he'd build a place where he could walk around and be by himself."

Her eyes smarted. "Well he certainly accomplished that here."

"Yeah. I love it. Our house in Athens is old and full of people all the time, too."

Stella hadn't ever thought about it before, but he was right. Rich or poor, both her family and Theo's had been through a lot of togetherness.

As they rounded a small headland, her feet came to a stop. This was the little cove where Theo always brought her in the rowboat. This was where they'd made passionate love for the first time. Ari had been conceived here.

She lifted wet eyes to capture the scene. In the distance she saw the man she loved hunkered down on the sand in shorts and a T-shirt, watching the ocean. This part of the coast was protected, making the water as calm as a lake.

"Papa!"

He turned his head. By the way he slowly got to his feet she could tell he was shocked to see her with Ari.

Her heart pounded so hard, it seemed to give her wings as she started running toward him. Suddenly he was galvanized into action and raced toward her as if he could outrun the wind. They met halfway and clung in euphoric rapture while he swung her around.

"Darling," she cried breathlessly.

Theo didn't speak words she could hear. He did it with his mouth, covering hers hungrily, letting her know how he felt while they communicated in the way they used to when they found this special spot to be together.

"Thank God you came," he whispered at last. "I swear I—"

"Shh." She pressed her lips to his. "We're never going to talk about this again. We're never going to think about the past again. Don't look now, but I think we've embarrassed our son."

When Theo lifted his dark head, the last rays of the sun gilded his features. They were more striking to her now than ever before. His black eyes devoured her before shifting to their son, who stood a little ways off watching a sailboat in the distance.

"Ari? You'll have to forgive your mother and me. She just told me she'd marry me."

"You did?" He shrieked for joy.

She nodded.

"That's so awesome, Mom!" He leaped in the air, shouting like a maniac. His whole face was wet from happy tears. Her heart thrilled to see the smile that transformed him.

"'So awesome' is right," Theo murmured, kissing her again. "I kind of lost control for a minute."

Ari laughed and ran over to them. They all hugged for a long time.

"How soon is the wedding?"

"Three weeks," they both said at the same time. He smiled into her eyes. "That should give us enough time."

"Why do you have to wait so long?"

She slid her arm around their son. "The wedding banns."

"What are those?"

"An announcement that we're getting married," Theo explained. "It gives anyone time to object if they know a reason why we shouldn't be married."

"That's crazy! Who wouldn't want you two to get married?"

Stella's eyes sought Theo's. The moment was bittersweet until he said, "Nobody I know, and you're absolutely right. It *is* crazy, but it's tradition. Come on. Let's go back to the house and plan the wedding."

"Are you going to ask Hektor to marry you?"

"Who else?" Theo teased.

"Are you guys going to go on a honeymoon?"

That forlorn little tone had sneaked into his voice. Theo smiled at her before he said, "We're thinking either Disneyland or Disney World. We'll let you make the decision."

"Disneyland!" he cried out. "Dax said it's awesome!"

# CHAPTER TEN

*Eleven Months Later*

"RACHEL? Would you do me a favor?" She and Stella were lying by the pool at the villa on Andros looking at baby magazines.

"What is it?"

"Don't look now but Theo's staring at me from the other end of the patio. My due date isn't for another three days, but you'd think I was on the verge of giving birth right now. Tell Stasio to take him somewhere for the day. I swear if he hovers around me one more minute, I'm going to scream."

"I know exactly how you feel. Stasio drove me crazy for the last couple of weeks before Anna was born."

"I'm getting there fast."

"He's in the house changing her diaper. As soon as he comes out, I'll ask him."

"Thank you."

"Uh-oh."

"What?"

"Theo's coming over here."

Stella lifted the magazine higher, pretending not to see him.

"You've been in the sun long enough, Stella. Let's get you inside for a little while. Too much heat isn't good for you."

"I haven't been out here that long."

"I disagree." In the next breath he picked her up off the lounge with those strong arms and carried her in the house to their bedroom.

Once he'd placed her carefully on top of the bed, he lay down next to her and smoothed the hair off her forehead. The anxious concern in his eyes baffled her.

"Darling, I'm as healthy as a horse. You don't need to worry about me. When I was carrying Ari, I never had any trouble. There's no reason to believe I'll have it this time."

"But I wasn't there to take care of you. Now that we can enjoy this spring break with the family, I want to wait on you."

"I know, and I love you for it, but watching me all the time is like waiting for water to boil."

His lips twitched. "Not quite. You're much more interesting." His hand slid over the mound, sending delicious chills through her body. "Is she kicking right now?"

"Not at the moment. I'll let you know the second she does. Come on. Close your eyes and take a little nap with me."

"That's kind of hard when I want to do more than that with you."

"I think you've done quite enough for one year, Kyrie Pantheras."

He chuckled deep in his throat and bit gently on her earlobe. "You're a fertile little thing."

"So I've found out. We're going to have to be careful after she's born."

His dark brows furrowed. "Is that your way of telling me the honeymoon's over?"

"No." She grabbed his hand and kissed his fingertips. "It's my way of telling you we could probably have a baby every year for the next ten years without a problem."

"I like the idea in theory."

"You would. You're not the one who feels like a walrus."

He grinned. "Yesterday it was a hippo. A very sexy one, I might add."

"Oh, Theo." She cupped his cheeks. "I love you too much."

Their mouths fused for a long time. "Now you know how I feel all the time."

"Pretty soon this baby will be born and you can stop worrying."

She heard his sharp intake of breath. "If anything happened to you—"

"It's not going to," she said.

"Have I told you Ari's latest idea for a name?"

"No. What is it?"

"We were looking at the Andromeda constellation the other night and he said, 'Papa? Can we name the baby Andrea?'"

"That's a beautiful name."

"I like it, too."

"Then let's do it. Ari will be thrilled."

"We'll tell him later. Right now I have other plans for us. Roll over on your side and I'll give you a back rub."

"That sounds heavenly." She'd had a low backache all week. It was the pressure of the baby since it had dropped.

The second Theo began touching her, her body quickened. Slowly his caresses sent sparks of desire through her, making her breathless. His mouth played havoc with hers. Stella wanted him with a need so powerful it turned into literal pain. She must have let out a little cry.

"What's wrong?"

"Nothing that a night of making love without our baby separating us won't cure."

"I probably shouldn't be touching you at all."

"If you didn't, I don't know how I'd go on living." She pressed her mouth to his and clung. All of a sudden she felt another pain that came all the way around to her stomach.

She grabbed Theo's hand and put it there. "Feel how hard that is?"

"Like a rock."

"I'm in labor, darling."

"You're kidding!" His voice shook.

"No. This is how it started before. We'd better call the doctor."

His face drained of color, Theo rolled off the bed and pulled out his cell phone. "His number's there on the bed stand."

The next few minutes were a blur while she timed her contractions. "They're coming every five minutes."

She didn't hear what Theo was saying, but after he got off the phone he told her they were leaving for the hospital. "The doctor says the baby could come fast because this isn't your first. Come on. We'll take Stasio's car."

"That's right," she quipped. "This beached whale couldn't get inside my sports car right now."

The joke was lost on Theo, who looked absolutely terrified. He helped her down the hall and the steps, calling to Stasio, who came running. By now the whole family had gathered around the car.

Rachel leaned inside the window. "I'll take care of the boys. Theo will take care of you. Don't worry about a thing."

It didn't take long to reach the hospital in Palaiopolis. She hadn't planned to have her baby there, but then you never knew what a baby was going to do. Andrea wanted to be born now.

Two and a half hours later she heard a gurgling sound and the attending doctor lifted up their little girl who was crying her lungs out. Knowing they were working and healthy meant everything.

"You've got a strong, beautiful daughter here, Kyrie Pantheras. Here—you cut the cord."

Theo, who'd put on a hospital gown and gloves, let out a cry of happiness. He'd lived through every second of the last few hours with her. Stella's tears ran down the sides of her cheeks. He hadn't been a part of any of this before. She was so thankful he had the opportunity now, she couldn't contain her joy.

A minute later the doctor laid the baby across her stomach so she could see her. "She's got a little widow's peak just like yours, darling!"

"She's got your hair and mouth."

"Oh, she's so sweet."

Theo buried his face in Stella's neck. "My two girls." She could tell he was overcome with emotion. She was, too, but so exhausted from the birth and filled with love for her new family, she could feel herself drifting off.

When next Stella came awake, she was in a private room. Theo stood at the side of the bed holding their daughter, who was all cleaned up and bundled. Her father had a five-o'clock shadow and his black hair was disheveled. Theo made a gorgeous sight!

Their gazes collided.

"You're awake!"

She smiled. "Yes. What do you think of our little girl?"

"Words don't cover it," his voice trembled.

"I know."

He lowered Andrea into her arms, then sat on a stool next to her. Together they examined their baby. "I've already checked everything. She's perfect."

Stella broke down laughing. "She is."

Theo covered Stella's face with kisses. "How are you feeling?"

"Good. Like I'm floating."

"You women are the stronger sex. I know that now." His eyes were pleading with her. "You've given me the world. What can I give you?"

"Just go on loving me. I need you desperately. I always will."

The baby started fussing. "She's hungry."

"She sure is," the nurse's voice boomed. "You'll have to leave for about a half hour while I help your wife start to nurse, Kyrie Pantheras."

He lowered his mouth to hers once more. "I'll be back."

"We'll be here waiting."

Theo drove back to the villa in record time. Ari and Leandros were waiting for him. "You have a new sister. We decided to name her Andrea."

He grinned. "Hooray. Can I go see her?"

"As soon as I've showered and shaved."

"Can I go, too, Uncle Theo?"

"Of course. Anyone who wants to."

"We'll all go." Stasio brought up the rear.

Ten minutes later they all piled in the car and left for the hospital. When they reached Stella's room, she was lying there propped up in the bed with the baby asleep on her shoulder. For a woman who'd given birth such a short time ago, Theo found his wife utterly breathtaking.

While everyone had a chance to hold the baby, he moved over to her side. "You must be exhausted, yet you've never looked more alive."

"That's because you were with me. We're the luckiest people in the world to be given a second chance at life. Oh, Theo…it was worth the six-year wait."

Theo had a hard time swallowing. "I can say that, now that you're alive and safe, but I wouldn't recommend it for everyone."

"No."

Unable to resist, he kissed her thoroughly. "I know there's a part of you that wishes Nikos could be here. One day let's hope he can find our kind of happiness and come around again."

Her eyes filled with liquid. "You can say that after everything he did to you?"

"I've forgotten it. It's true what they say. Love really does heal all wounds."

"Theo…"

"Hey, Mom? She kind of looks like Cassie except she doesn't have red hair."

"Do you know something, Ari, honey? Every day you look at her, you're going to see someone else in the family she looks like. It's part of being a baby."

"She's cute."

"Of course she is," said Theo. "I'm her father!"

Ari laughed. "Did you hear that, Mom?"

"I heard it."

Theo had come back to Greece not expecting to claim her or their son. Instead he had both and their adorable Andrea. That was her joy and her blessing.

* * * * *

*Celebrate 60 years of pure reading pleasure
with Harlequin®!*

To commemorate the event, Silhouette Special
Edition invites you to Ashley O'Ballivan's bed-
and-breakfast in the small town of Stone Creek.
The beautiful innkeeper will have her hands full
caring for her old flame Jack McCall. He's on the
run and recovering from a mysterious illness, but
that won't stop him from trying to win Ashley back.

*Enjoy an exclusive glimpse of Linda Lael Miller's
AT HOME IN STONE CREEK
Available in November 2009
from Silhouette Special Edition®*

The helicopter swung abruptly sideways in a dizzying arch, setting Jack McCall's fever-ravaged brain spinning.

His friend's voice sounded tinny, coming through the earphones. "You belong in a hospital," he said. "Not some backwater bed-and-breakfast."

All Jack really knew about the virus raging through his system was that it wasn't contagious, and there was no known treatment for it besides a lot of rest and quiet. "I don't like hospitals," he responded, hoping he sounded like his normal self. "They're full of sick people."

Vince Griffin chuckled but it was a dry sound, rough at the edges. "What's in Stone Creek, Arizona?" he asked. "Besides a whole lot of nothin'?"

Ashley O'Ballivan was in Stone Creek, and she was a whole lot of somethin', but Jack had neither the strength nor the inclination to explain. After the way he'd ducked out six months before, he didn't expect a welcome, knew he didn't deserve one. But Ashley, being Ashley, would take him in whatever her misgivings.

He had to get to Ashley; he'd be all right.

He closed his eyes, letting the fever swallow him.

There was no telling how much time had passed

when he became aware of the chopper blades slowing overhead. Dimly, he saw the private ambulance waiting on the airfield outside of Stone Creek; it seemed that twilight had descended.

Jack sighed with relief. His clothes felt clammy against his flesh. His teeth began to chatter as two figures unloaded a gurney from the back of the ambulance and waited for the blades to stop.

"Great," Vince remarked, unsnapping his seat belt. "Those two look like volunteers, not real EMTs."

The chopper bounced sickeningly on its runners, and Vince, with a shake of his head, pushed open his door and jumped to the ground, head down.

Jack waited, wondering if he'd be able to stand on his own. After fumbling unsuccessfully with the buckle on his seat belt, he decided not.

When it was safe the EMTs approached, following Vince, who opened Jack's door.

His old friend Tanner Quinn stepped around Vince, his grin not quite reaching his eyes.

"You look like hell warmed over," he told Jack cheerfully.

"Since when are you an EMT?" Jack retorted.

Tanner reached in, wedged a shoulder under Jack's right arm and hauled him out of the chopper. His knees immediately buckled, and Vince stepped up, supporting him on the other side.

"In a place like Stone Creek," Tanner replied, "everybody helps out."

They reached the wheeled gurney, and Jack found himself on his back.

Tanner and the second man strapped him down, a process that brought back a few bad memories.

"Is there even a hospital in this place?" Vince asked irritably from somewhere in the night.

"There's a pretty good clinic over in Indian Rock," Tanner answered easily, "and it isn't far to Flagstaff." He paused to help his buddy hoist Jack and the gurney into the back of the ambulance. "You're in good hands, Jack. My wife is the best veterinarian in the state."

Jack laughed raggedly at that.

Vince muttered a curse.

Tanner climbed into the back beside him, perched on some kind of fold-down seat. The other man shut the doors.

"You in any pain?" Tanner said as his partner climbed into the driver's seat and started the engine.

"No." Jack looked up at his oldest and closest friend and wished he'd listened to Vince. Ever since he'd come down with the virus—a week after snatching a five-year-old girl back from her non-custodial parent, a small-time Colombian drug dealer—he hadn't been able to think about anyone or anything but Ashley. When he *could* think, anyway.

Now, in one of the first clearheaded moments he'd experienced since checking himself out of Bethesda the day before, he realized he might be making a major mistake. Not by facing Ashley—he owed her that much and a lot more. No, he could be putting her in danger, putting Tanner and his daughter and his pregnant wife in danger, too.

"I shouldn't have come here," he said, keeping his voice low.

Tanner shook his head, his jaw clamped down hard as though he was irritated by Jack's statement.

"This is where you belong," Tanner insisted. "If

you'd had sense enough to know that six months ago, old buddy, when you bailed on Ashley without so much as a fare-thee-well, you wouldn't be in this mess."

*Ashley.* The name had run through his mind a million times in those six months, but hearing somebody say it out loud was like having a fist close around his insides and squeeze hard.

Jack couldn't speak.

Tanner didn't press for further conversation.

The ambulance bumped over country roads, finally hitting smooth blacktop.

"Here we are," Tanner said. "Ashley's place."

* * * * *

*Will Jack be able to patch things up with Ashley,
or will his past put the woman he loves
in harm's way?
Find out in
AT HOME IN STONE CREEK
by Linda Lael Miller
Available November 2009
from Silhouette Special Edition®*

This November,
**Silhouette Special Edition®**
brings you

*NEW YORK TIMES*
BESTSELLING AUTHOR

# LINDA LAEL MILLER

*At Home in*
## Stone Creek

*Available in November
wherever books are sold.*

# HARLEQUIN® Romance®

*This November,
queen of the rugged rancher*

# PATRICIA THAYER

*teams up with*

# DONNA ALWARD

*to bring you an extra-special treat
this holiday season—*

## two romantic stories
## in one book!

Join sisters Amelia and Kelley for Christmas at
Rocking H Ranch where these feisty cowgirls swap
presents for proposals, mistletoe for marriage and
experience the unbeatable rush of falling in love!

*Available in November wherever books are sold.*

**www.eHarlequin.com**

HRI7619

# nocturne™

## TIME RAIDERS
# THE PROTECTOR

by *USA TODAY* bestselling author
# MERLINE LOVELACE

Former USAF officer Cassandra Jones's unique psychic
skills come in handy, as she has been selected to join the
elite Time Raiders squad. Her first mission is to travel
back to seventh-century China to locate the final piece
of a missing bronze medallion. Major Max Brody is
assigned to accompany her, and soon Cassandra and
Max have to fight their growing attraction to each
other while the mission suddenly turns deadly....

*Available November
wherever books are sold.*

www.silhouettenocturne.com
www.paranormalromanceblog.com

SN61822

# REQUEST YOUR FREE BOOKS!
## 2 FREE NOVELS PLUS 2
# FREE GIFTS!

HARLEQUIN®

*Romance*®

## From the Heart, For the Heart

---

**YES!** Please send me 2 FREE Harlequin® Romance novels and my 2 FREE gifts (gifts are worth about $10). After receiving them, if I don't wish to receive any more books, I can return the shipping statement marked "cancel". If I don't cancel, I will receive 4 brand-new novels every month and be billed just $3.84 per book in the U.S. or $4.24 per book in Canada. That's a savings of at least 15% off the cover price! It's quite a bargain! Shipping and handling is just 50¢ per book.* I understand that accepting the 2 free books and gifts places me under no obligation to buy anything. I can always return a shipment and cancel at any time. Even if I never buy another book, the two free books and gifts are mine to keep forever.

114 HDN EYU3  314 HDN EYKG

| | |
|---|---|
| Name | (PLEASE PRINT) |

| | |
|---|---|
| Address | Apt. # |

| | | |
|---|---|---|
| City | State/Prov. | Zip/Postal Code |

Signature (if under 18, a parent or guardian must sign)

Mail to the **Harlequin Reader Service:**
**IN U.S.A.:** P.O. Box 1867, Buffalo, NY 14240-1867
**IN CANADA:** P.O. Box 609, Fort Erie, Ontario L2A 5X3

Not valid to current subscribers of Harlequin Romance books.

**Are you a subscriber of Harlequin Romance books
and want to receive the larger-print edition?
Call 1-800-873-8635 today!**

\* Terms and prices subject to change without notice. Prices do not include applicable taxes. Sales tax applicable in N.Y. Canadian residents will be charged applicable provincial taxes and GST. Offer not valid in Quebec. This offer is limited to one order per household. All orders subject to approval. Credit or debit balances in a customer's account(s) may be offset by any other outstanding balance owed by or to the customer. Please allow 4 to 6 weeks for delivery. Offer available while quantities last.

**Your Privacy:** Harlequin Books is committed to protecting your privacy. Our Privacy Policy is available online at www.eHarlequin.com or upon request from the Reader Service. From time to time we make our lists of customers available to reputable third parties who may have a product or service of interest to you. If you would prefer we not share your name and address, please check here. ☐

HR09R

# HARLEQUIN
## *Ambassadors*

### *Want to share your passion for reading Harlequin® Books?*

## Become a Harlequin Ambassador!

Harlequin Ambassadors are a group of passionate and well-connected readers who are willing to share their joy of reading Harlequin® books with family and friends.

You'll be sent all the tools you need to spark great conversation, including free books!

All we ask is that you share the romance with your friends and family!

You'll also be invited to have a say in new book ideas and exchange opinions with women just like you!

**To see if you qualify\* to be a Harlequin Ambassador, please visit www.HarlequinAmbassadors.com.**

\*Please note that not everyone who applies to be a Harlequin Ambassador will qualify. For more information please visit www.HarlequinAmbassadors.com.

**Thank you for your participation.**

BAP09BPA

## Coming Next Month

### Available November 10, 2009

**For an early surprise this Christmas don't look under the Christmas tree or in your stocking—look out for *Christmas Treats* in your November Harlequin® Romance novels!**

#### #4129 MONTANA, MISTLETOE, MARRIAGE
*Christmas Treats*
**Patricia Thayer and Donna Alward**
Join sisters Amelia and Kelley for Christmas on Rocking H Ranch as we bring you two stories in one volume for double the romance!

#### #4130 THE MAGIC OF A FAMILY CHRISTMAS  Susan Meier
*Christmas Treats*
All six-year-old Harry wants for Christmas is for his new mom, Wendy, to marry so they can be a forever family. Will his wish come true?

#### #4131 CROWNED: THE PALACE NANNY  Marion Lennox
*Marrying His Majesty*
When powerful prince Stefanos meets feisty nanny Elsa, sparks fly! But will she ever agree to *Marrying His Majesty*? Find out in the final installment of this majestic trilogy.

#### #4132 CHRISTMAS ANGEL FOR THE BILLIONAIRE  Liz Fielding
*Trading Places*
Lady Rosanne Napier is *Trading Places* with a celebrity look-alike to escape the spotlight and meets the man of her dreams in the start of this brand-new duet.

#### #4133 COWBOY DADDY, JINGLE-BELL BABY  Linda Goodnight
*Christmas Treats*
On a dusty Texas roadside, cowboy Dax delivers Jenna's baby. When he offers her a job, neither expects her to become his housekeeper bride!

#### #4134 UNDER THE BOSS'S MISTLETOE  Jessica Hart
*Christmas Treats*
Cassie was determined to ignore the attraction she felt for her new boss, but that was before she was forced to pose under the mistletoe with delectable Jake!